ONLY GOD CAN CREATE A WOMAN

A Novel by
RODNEY E. DANIELS

Published by Rodney E Daniels
a division of reddot media group.
www.reddotmediagroup.com

ISBN 978-0-9760466-9-5

This novel is a work of fiction. Names, characters, places and incidents are a product of the author's imagination. Any resemblance to actual persons, living or dead, places, events or locales are strictly coincidental and intended to provide the fiction work with a sense of authenticity.

Printed in the United States of America

Acknowledgements

First and foremost, special thanks to my Lord and Savior, Jesus Christ. Through him all things are possible.

A special thanks to my niece, LaShawn Daniels, for always being there when I needed someone. I could never repay you for your generosity. To Evelyn George, for all of your support throughout the years. To all of my family and friends for being there through all of my hard times.

To everyone who was involved throughout the entire process of putting this project together: John Gore and Ishmael Naveras for proofreading and reviewing this work. Thank you to Tiffany Davis and Tiyauna Williams your editorial expertise. Thank you, Jeannette Mobley, for bringing my ideas to life in the cover design. To Clarence Cunningham and Stacey Sterling for typing and retyping the manuscript every time I found a mistake.

Thanks to Sharon Belizairo for being there when I needed someone to talk to.

Special thanks to my mother, father and host of sisters for everything.

If I speak in the tongues of men and of angels, but have not love I am only a resounding gong or a clanging cymbal. If I have the gift of prophecy and can fathom all mysteries and all knowledge, and if I have faith that can move mountains, but have not love, I am nothing. If I give all I possess to the poor and surrender my body to the flames, but have not love I gain nothing.

Love is patient, love is kind. It does not envy; it does not boast; it is not proud. It is not rude, it is not self-seeking, it is not easily angered; it keeps no record of wrongs. Love does not delight in evil but rejoices with the truth. It always protects, always trusts, always hopes, and always perseveres.

Love never fails.

I Corinthians 13:1-8a

Chapter 1

They say hell has no fury like a woman scorned but I don't know what I did to this woman. I haven't seen her in four years but here I am, sitting in court, about to be sentenced to three years in jail for tax fraud. And this seems to be the happiest day of her life and after everything I've done for her- Ms. Leslie Simmons- that ungrateful bitch. Every time I looked behind me she sported a wicked smile. She and her twin sister, Lisa, dressed exactly alike.

Leslie had a deep caramel complexion, very smooth skin and the most flawless radiant hazel eyes with a hint of green around the edges. Her hair was a little past her shoulders with light brown highlights. She was one of the most beautiful women I've ever known, but also one of the dumbest. Maybe dumb is the wrong word; let's just say she was socially unconscious.

But now I realized she was not as dumb as I thought. She was the mastermind behind all of the trouble I'm in now.

I met Leslie at Diamond's Gym. She was wearing extra-tight biker shorts and a sports bra. As she walked out of the women's dressing room, I spotted her and thanked God because I had never seen a woman more beautiful than her. She headed over to the treadmill and I ran behind her, cutting off another woman; well actually, I pushed the other woman out of the way to get to the treadmill next to Leslie. After programming the treadmill and starting my slight jog, I searched for the right words to say but my mind kept coming up blank. I was at a loss for words. She must have noticed my agony because she turned to me, stared at me for about thirty seconds and said, "Yes, I will go out with you." At first I was relieved, but then immediately became defensive.

"Excuse me?" I asked.

She looked at me and smiled.

"I know what you want. First, you stared at me so hard when I came out of the dressing room; I practically felt your eyes massaging my breasts. Then you tackle the poor old lady to get to this treadmill next to me. Then you began arguing with yourself, I assume trying to find the right words. So I just decided to help you out. Yes, I will go out with you. How about Friday? You can pick me up at Total Experience Beauty Salon around eight o'clock. And by the way, my name is Leslie."

I attempted to shake her hand and stumbled. I almost fell off the treadmill, but being the overconfident man that I am; I went into a faster run and recovered quickly. After a few seconds I stopped the treadmill and finally shook her hand.

"My name is…" Damn! I temporarily forgot my name. It took a few seconds but I finally spit it out.

"Darius, Darius Miller."

We both laughed. My recovery was good but it hadn't fooled anyone. I held Leslie's hand a little longer than necessary but they were soft. I also had to check for a ring, or at least the shadow of a ring. There was none. I let her hand go slowly. I glanced at her nails—not too long. Perfect. Well taken care of with a classic French manicure. I wanted to look at the palms of her hands to see if they were tips but that would have been push-ing it.

"Okay, Leslie that Total Experience Beauty Salon, if I'm correct, is on Linden Boulevard in Cambria Heights, right?

"Yes," Leslie smiled, showing me her pearly white teeth which seemed to sparkle like the old Dentyne commercial. She had me hooked. I glanced at the clock and saw that is was twelve-thirty. Damn, I was running late. I had a meeting in one hour but didn't want to leave her presence. I cleared my throat.

"Why don't you give me your number so I can confirm every-thing Thursday night?"

"No. If you want to see me, pick me up at eight on Friday—and don't be late." She smirked.

I shook my head. "Okay, Friday at eight. I'll be there."

1.

Chapter 2

I pushed old Patsy to the limit because I didn't want to be late. Patsy was my aquamarine 1989 Honda Accord with tan interior and Pirelli tires that were set on chrome five-star rims. Even at thirteen years old, she was my baby. If I met a woman while driving this car, I knew she wanted me for me and not my money. When it comes to money, I hold on tighter than a virgin with an attitude. I also own a Mercedes Benz CLK 500 convertible, but I keep that at home most of the time. I don't need people thinking I have a lot of money. but I do all right.

Traffic was light for a change on the Long Island Expressway, which was unusual at any time of the day. I was able to make it on time. This meeting was very important for my business, so (CPT) "Colored People Time" was not an option. I called myself a subterranean engineer, which was a fancy title I came up with. Basically, I clean sewers and drain lines via Roto

Rooter. It's not very glamorous but I make as much as some Fortune 500 company executives. I have little overhead, ten trucks, five phone lines and fifteen workers. If I can get this contract, it would double my business instantly. Looking at my Rolex, I noticed I had plenty of time. My exit was coming up next.

Thoughts of Leslie consumed my mind. Her breasts and the way they bounced up and down while she was on the treadmill looked like they were waving at me: "Hi Darius!" Her legs were shapely; lips, plump and kissable. She was perfect in every way. I was startled out of my fantasy by blowing car horns and my ringing cell phone. Shit! I was holding up traffic thinking about this chick.

Somehow I made it to my destination. Damn that phone!

"Atomic Sewer and Drain Cleaning. Darius Miller speaking. May I help you?"

"Darius?"

Oh God. Not now.

"Darius, it's me, Brenda," she said, as if I wouldn't have recognized her annoying ass.

"Brenda, this is not a good time. I'm on my way to a meeting."

"Call me back as soon as your meeting is over. I need you to take DJ for the weekend. I'm going to Atlantic City and it's your weekend. If you can pick him up on Friday instead of Saturday, I'll be grateful."

"Sure. No problem." Then I thought about Leslie. "NO! Wait, I can't. I have plans this Friday night."

"Darius, please! Do me this favor."

"Brenda, as much as I love my son, you can't keep doing this to me. That shit you pulled last weekend was crazy. How could you just leave DJ outside my apartment with an overnight bag? What if I didn't come home? Did you forget that he's only four years old? Brenda, you need to get your shit together and stop with the bullshit. If the guy you are around doesn't want DJ around, then you should leave him. If he can't accept the fact that you have a child, you don't need to be with him."

"Darius, I didn't call to argue with you."

"Good, because I don't have the time right now. I'll call you later." I hung up before she could utter another word.

Brenda wasn't a bad person and she's a pretty good mother. I'm not going to let her know that I saw her across the street from my apartment last week sitting in her boyfriend's car. Dropping Darius Jr. off at my apartment with an overnight bag and a note is not the way to handle things. I know I hurt her, even though she would never admit it. I'm sorry for it but when it comes to my son, I must protect him. Brenda and I can't seem to meet on common ground on some things. She was never my type. All of it just happened.

I was at a friend's house playing cards. His wife was always trying to hook me up with someone. In walks Brenda, 5'6", medium brown complexion, very nice breasts, but her ass was flat. Finding a black woman with no ass is like invading Europe and finding they ran out of white women, and that shit's not going to happen. But it didn't stop me because I can find beauty in anyone. We played cards for a while and talked. Brenda explained to me that she had just come out of an eight-year relationship that was very abusive. I didn't know if I felt sorry for her or if it was the alcohol, but I offered her a ride home. We stopped at a diner, talked some more over cheese-burgers and fries and went back to her apartment, and things lead on from there. The next morning we went at it again but I told myself that after I left I'd never see her again, and kept it that way for weeks.

Then one day, I came home after work and she was sitting in front of my apartment, crying. I felt sorry for her again and sat down next to her. We talked for almost two hours. Then I let her in, told her to have a seat and that I needed to take a shower. I wasn't in the shower long but by the time I got out Brenda was in her bra and panties in my kitchen, cooking. I should have thrown her ass out right then and there because I knew she had game. She handed me a beer, yanked the towel from around my waist, pushed me back onto the couch, and proceeded to give me the best head I ever had to this day. I mean, she didn't miss a spot! My toes curled up tighter than a fist. I almost pulled up the carpet. I arched my back, dropped my beer, and pushed her head back down. Brenda gagged, stopped, looked up at me and says, "I got this, baby. I want to taste your juices."

That was the corniest shit I ever heard but I didn't care. Shit, she almost had me speaking in tongues. I damn near wanted to sing. Head is all right but I love intercourse more and right then and there she changed that. I arched my back further and I knew she had me hooked. Right then my eyes rolled up in the back of my head while very muscle in my body was clenched. I was wound up tighter than a spinning top. I mean, every hair on my body was standing at attention. I felt a light—a bright light-envelop my eyes. I was blinded with sheer ecstasy as I exploded!

BEEP! BEEP! Damn, I was lost thinking about Brenda. Another car wanted my parking spot but I waved the driver off. I reached under my seat, grabbed the bottle of Cool Water cologne, put on a drop so as not to overdo it, snatched up my briefcase and ran for the building. Six minutes to get to the third floor. I pressed the elevator button and waited in the lobby, checking myself in the full-length mirror. My Italian-cut suit hung great on my 6'2" frame. My goatee, freshly trimmed; brown eyes, clear and bright. I noticed a few lines under my eyes but I'm thirty-six and could still pass for twenty-nine or thirty. My baldhead had a nice shine to it to I let people know I'm bald by razor and not by nature. I didn't have any gray hairs on my body. As I stepped into the elevator, I almost forgot to take out my earrings. Definitely not business like.

The lobby was not what I expected. These buildings were new but the furniture must have been twenty years old. The carpet was a cheap commercial brown with runs in it, meaning it was so

15

worn that it was pulling apart in many places. I thought the lobby was the showroom of the company, if so, than it was apparent that someone was being real cheap. To the right was a multicolor brown tweed couch on wooden legs with a matching love seat and an old coffee table filled with magazines. To the left was the receptionist and straight ahead were some dusty plastic plants. The receptionist was an old white-haired woman in a plain creamed-colored suit wearing a pearl necklace with matching earrings.

"Sir, may I help you?"

I was still taking in the tackiness of the place. She passed me a clipboard, thinking I was here to fill out an application.

"Sir?"

I snapped to attention. "No, Ma'am. My name is Darius Miller. I'm here to see Ms. Drake."

"Oh yes, Mr. Miller. Have a seat. She'll be right with you."

I walked over the couch, sat down, and almost fell to the floor. The springs in the couch were busted and I literally broke into a sweat just swimming out of that hole. I looked at the receptionist and she just looked back with a smile on her face. I looked back at the couch and noticed it had bounced back into place, waiting for its next victim.

"Hello, Mr. Miller. Nice to see you again."

I turned around and Marcia Drake was behind me, smiling. I shook her hand.

"How are you? Nice to see you again, Ms. Drake."

"I'm doing fine, Mr. Miller. May I call you Darius? It's not like we haven't met socially already. Let's go to my office."

Marcia wore a dark blue business suit. The skirt wasn't much longer than the jacket and the jacket was cut low to show ample cleavage. Marcia is about 5'9", blonde, blue eyes, and very nicely shaped. The diamond pendant was a nice touch with the matching earrings but her eyes seemed to glow brighter than the diamonds.

Her office and the lobby looked like they belong in two separate buildings. Her desk was a large, ornately designed cherry wood with gold knobs. The leather captain's chair was also a nice touch. The paintings on the wall looked very expensive to me. I thought they were real Picassos. The carpet was so thick, I felt like I was walking on clouds.

"Have a seat."

She pointed to a very dark red leather couch.

"Don't worry. This one won't eat you."

I smiled and took a seat.

"Darius, I haven't seen you since the Johnson's party. I even stopped by your house twice. Mrs. Mary Johnson says you don't spend much time there. I wanted to have you sign the contract there and save all the formality."

"I'm sorry. I don't spend much time at my house, except week-ends. I don't know why I even bought it. I spend most of my week in Queens. Mary told me it's just a waste to keep that lovely home empty so much."

Marcia's intercom buzzed. She answered it and excused herself.

I met Ms. Marcia Drake at a house party given by my next-door neighbors, John and Mary Johnson. John is black, so black that he looks navy blue. Mary, on the other hand was white. I mean, house paint white. To see them together is like looking at an x-ray or piano keys. The contrast in color is mind blowing. If they had kids, I swear to you that they would come out gray. John owns a lot of buildings in Queens and Brooklyn that I service from time to time. That's why he introduced me to Marcia Drake: she owns and manages about 100 buildings throughout Brooklyn, Queens, and Manhattan. The night of the party, Marcia was all over me. She's a very attractive rich woman but I'm not O.J. Simpson and to me, white just ain't right.

Before I noticed Marcia was back in the office, my mind had drifted off to Leslie again. Then something struck me in an instant, about what just occurred. Oh, no, this bitch thinks she's Sharon Stone. Marcia didn't have any panties on!

Darius I looked over your proposal and I think we can do business."

She smiled and opened her legs wider so I could get a better look. Now I knew she wasn't a natural blonde because the "collar" didn't match the cuffs.

"Darius, take care of me and I will take care of you." Her skirt rose higher and she started massaging herself. "Eat me, Darius."

What! This bitch was crazy. I wasn't selling my soul to the devil. I didn't care how much business she could throw my way.

"Marcia, I'm sorry. I don't mix business with pleasure. It would never work out," I said confidently, but still in a state of shock.

Marcia pulled her skirt down.

"Mr. Miller, I think you should leave."

I picked up my briefcase and walked to the door. Before I opened it she was back at the desk, about to pick up the phone. When I walked out I thought I heard her call me a homo. I was about to respond but changed my mind. I'm not selling out for any amount of money and if I argued with her, I was definitely going to jail. Best to leave well enough alone, plus, I tried that white interracial dating scene once- and once was enough. The looks I got from black women everywhere we went made me feel like I let down every black woman on the planet.

Chapter 3

It's Friday and two things have dominated my mind all week. One was Marcia, rubbing herself, asking me to taste her. She's not a bad-looking woman and her being extremely wealthy didn't hurt matters but I knew if anything happened, I would be in her debt and I'm my own man.

Second, was Leslie's beauty? I'm not a shallow brother and looks aren't everything but it's a damn good start. If I could have gotten her phone number, tonight would be much easier. I could have found out her likes and dislikes so that planning this night would have been much simpler, no matter what. I knew everything would be all right though, thanks to my connections. I loved my job and I know it isn't glamorous but it pays well and I'm the boss. My client list was extensive. Not only did I serve apartment buildings and private homes but also some of the finest restaurants in New York City.

First thing this morning I sent Leslie two dozen African violets in some sort of fancy arrangement. They are supposed to be very expensive but I didn't know and I didn't care because I didn't pay for it. On Fourth Avenue and Flatbush was Vernon's florist. He was one of my oldest customers and he always has a problem with his drains clogging up in the flower refrigerator. He has to keep the flowers watered, so the drain must stay clean. Plus, I maintain the sprinkler system. So when I called this morning, Vernon was happy to donate the violets along with a dozen roses that I sent to Marcia Drake. I wanted her business, not her, so yellow roses should do the trick; they symbolized friendship. I wrote a letter because I didn't want to totally offend someone who regularly has lunch with the mayor.

After taking care of the flowers, I called Tavern on the Green, which is also a regular customer and one of my oldest. All I had to do was call the manager, John Stevens, and I was in. He made my guest and me feel like celebrities every time.

The last call I had to make this date perfect was to the Plaza Hotel. This was not a customer but an ex-girlfriend worked there and when someone goes to the Plaza and spends $5,000 a night for a room, and they want tickets to a sold-out show, then you better believe the Plaza is going to get tickets and private limo service for the night. So thanks to my friend, I had a limo for the night and tickets for The Lion King. To get tickets for that show and not have to order six months in advance, you had to be friends with the Pope and have God on your speed dial. So I hoped Leslie could appreciate everything I did for her. And because I was taking her to dinner and a Broadway show. I was not looking for sex but if she offered, I would damn sure take it. I would also be damn sure to wrap it up first. I know I was wrong but if I wanted some quick pussy, all I needed to do was call my son's mother, Brenda.

Chapter 4

I pulled up in front of Total Experience Beauty Salon at exactly 7:52pm. Leslie was talking to some guy out front. The smile on her face looked like she was enjoying the conversation. I couldn't get mad but it sort of hurt and I had to suck it up. She wasn't my girl yet and even if she were, I couldn't tell her whom to talk to or who her friends could be. That's what you have to expect with a beautiful woman: men always trying to get with her.

I looked in the rear view mirror. Damn! I looked good. My head was freshly shaved and, with my own special mixture of baby oil and pure cocoa butter, it stayed smooth with a slight shine. My goatee was freshly trimmed and I had two-carat diamond studs in both ears. Plus my dimples, when I did smile, usually drew women in like a deep pool, so I was ready. I stepped out of my truck. Yes, I drove my work truck. I don't know why I did. Maybe I just wanted to see how Leslie would react if she thought we were going out in a truck that said "Atomic Sewer and Drain Cleaning: Satisfaction guaranteed or Double Your Shit Back." I slammed the door, walked around the rear of the truck, put my foot on the bumper, took out a handkerchief and wiped off my gators. When I looked up, the guy Leslie was talking to eyed me up and down with a smirk on his face. Clearly he wasn't impressed with the truck. I adjusted the sleeve on my lightweight wool blend Prada suite and walked over with my hand extended to shake his.

"Hello, my name is Darius, nice to meet you." He shook my hand; actually, he tried to squeeze it while telling me his name was Juice. A grown man calling himself Juice? Yeah, OK. I then moved over to Leslie and kissed her on the check.
"You look beautiful."
She smiled and said, "Thank you, Darius. Give me one minute so I can grab my bag." As she walked away, she looked over her shoulder at me and said, "You're exactly on time. I'm impressed."
Juice and I both watched her walked into the salon.
"Damn! She's fine, ain't she Darius," Juice asked, still looking me over. "Nice truck..." he smirked again. He pulled out his keys; hit a button on the alarm which chirped on a three-year old 750 BMW.

"Nice BMW," I commented. He smiled and that's when I noticed the gold teeth.

Juice had to be about thirty-seven. He was wearing a white tank top, also known as a wife beater. He had well-built arms and upper chest, no doubt from hitting weights in whatever prison he was in because the jailhouse tattoo confirmed that fact. He was an average-looking brother but no real competition to me. Not like I'm the handsomest man in the world, but I'm damn sure not the ugliest. The polished silver chain with the cubic zirconium that he was trying to pass off as platinum and diamond; and the way his pants hung low confirmed my last thought: this brother still thinks he's still twenty-one. I called it the Peter Pan complex. Some men just refused to grow up.

Leslie walked up behind me and put her hand on my waist.

"Darius, I'm ready." We walked over to my truck. I opened the passenger door and reached in to grab my wallet off the seat. In the background I could hear Juice hit his alarm button again. I closed the passenger door.

"Darius? Leslie asked.

"Yes," I replied.

"Aren't we driving?"

"Sure," I said. "But not in this."

I pointed to the limo across the street. The driver was already by the back door, awaiting our arrival.

A reassuring smile spread across Leslie's pretty little face.

We crossed the street and I let Leslie slide in first. While I was getting in I could see the expression on Juice's face. First shock, then I'm not sure if the next look was jealousy or rage. I made a mental note that he may be trouble later. I also made a note to call one of my workers and remind him to move my truck.

The show was great. I could tell Leslie really enjoyed herself. She acted like a six-year old going to Disneyland for the first time. Another mental note: get tickets to another show. We walked out the door and the limo driver was again on hand.

I bowed to her. "My princess, your chariot awaits you." Then I took her hand and led her to the limo. I waited until she sat down and said, "Excuse me, Leslie. I need to use the phone."

I closed the door and leaned against it while I dialed the number. I noticed the window was open a crack but I acted like I didn't notice Leslie trying to listen.

"Hey, old lady." That was my term of endearment for my mother. She was nowhere near old as far as I was concerned but she likes to complain that she is so she can get more attention from me.

"How is DJ doing?" I asked.

"He's fine," she said. "Boy, what time are you picking him up in the morning, because I plan to go shopping with your sister?" I could hear the kids making noise in the background.

"You got the whole posse there tonight, huh, Mom? Why are they still up?" The posse consisted of DJ and my sister's two kids: Shana, who was six and the ringleader of the gang and Michael, who is five and wants to be the next world-wrestling champ.

"Well, they don't get together much. So I decided to let them tire themselves out when they do pass out, I can get a good night's sleep."

"Alright, old lady, if you think so. They will have you up until three in the morning. Okay, Ma, let me speak to DJ."

"Hi, Daddy," DJ said.

"Hey, DJ. Don't give Grandma any trouble. I'll see you in a little while."

"Daddy, Shana keeps grabbing the phone."

"Well, let me speak to her." There was a tussling sound, then Shana spoke.

"Hi, Uncle Darius." Mom says you were going out with one of your hoes and that I could spend the night with DJ. Uncle Darius, what's a hoe?"

"Shana, don't use that word. I'll explain it to you when I see you and tell your mother I need to talk to her. Now put Michael on the phone."

"Hi, Uncle Darius."

"Hey, Michael."

"Uncle Darius, The Rock is fighting Stone Cold next week. Can we go, please?"

"We'll see, Michael. Put your grandmother back on the phone."

When she picked up the receiver. I said, Ma, I have to go. Kiss the kids for me."

"Okay, baby. Have a good time and be safe."

I hung up the phone and was immediately questioned by Leslie.

"Who did you have to call, Mr. Miller, your girlfriend? She said with a smile. I wasn't even in the car yet. "So, what did she say?"

"One minute," I said. "I don't have a girlfriend." Leslie started laughing as soon as she saw how helpless I looked fumbling for the right words to say.

"You need to turn down the volume on your phone. I could hear every word they said and now I'm one of your hoes." She softened her words with a smile. I was really at loss for words but she let me off the hook again.

"I understand. Your sister wants you to find the right person and settle down. So when you get those wrestling tickets, I better get one too, to make up for being called a hoe. And I want to the see The Rock in person. He's one fine man." All I could do was smile. My posse had gotten me in trouble.

Chapter 5

We went to Tavern on the Green but some celebrity had showed up unexpectedly and the media was all over the place. However, I always have a back-up plan. So we went to Nino's, a small Italian restaurant on Court Street in downtown Brooklyn. Nino's is a mom-and-pop place. It had an old-fashioned flavor, or so I've been told, because I've never been to Italy. The tables were cozy with red and white-checkered tablecloths. The walls were adorned with signed photos of Frank Sinatra, Dean Martin and Marlon Brando from The Godfather and other people I didn't recognize. The floor held a high shine on solid oak planks. Over to the right was a long oak bar, well stocked, and on either side of it was the flag of Italy. Nino and his wife Maria opened this place in 1962 and it has been a fixture in the community ever since. Plus, the food was excellent.

Standing in the doorway was the first time I really noticed what Leslie was wearing. I was so busy observing her beauty and legs that I didn't notice her dress at all. I know she could have been wearing a potato sack and she still would have looked good. The black dress with the spaghetti straps cut low to her breasts was very provocative but not slutty. The bottom reached mid-thigh. She accented it all with a small black Prada purse and pumps. She wore a diamond pendant necklace and it turned me on because the diamond was wedged between her voluptuous breasts.

"Darius!" Maria greeted us. "Nice to see you again. How are you this evening?"

"I'm fine, thank you. Where is that husband of yours?"

"Oh, he's in the back. It's late and we were closing up. And who is this beautiful woman you're with?" Maria took Leslie by the hand, led her to a table and helped her with her chair. Before Leslie could say thank you, Marie was calling for her husband. Nino came in, wiping his hands on a towel.

"Darius, how nice to see you!"

I hugged Nino. "Good to see you too."

"Who's this beautiful woman you're with? He took Leslie's hand and kissed it.

"If I was twenty years younger, I'd steal you away from him," Nino said to Leslie.

Maria playfully tapped her husband on the back of his head. "If you were twenty years younger, you would still be twenty years too old for her."

That brought laughs from everyone.

"Darius, I have a special shrimp Parmigiana for you. It's so good. Let me make a special for you two, please."

Darius looked at Leslie. "Sure."

Nino turned to Maria. "Get Darius a bottle of our best wine."

While Nino and Maria prepared everything, I had a chance to talk to Leslie. "Leslie, I don't even know your last name. Tell me about yourself."

"What do you want to know, Darius?"

"Everything. Start with your last name."

"Well, my name is Leslie Anne Simmons and I have a twin sister named Lisa. I grew up in Queens Village. I have a normal life, nothing spectacular."

I smiled. "There has to be more than that. No friends? No boy-friend? Tell me.

Leslie gave me a skeptical look. "Are you trying to find out if I'm seeing anyone? Well, the answer is no. I'm not seeing any-one."

"What about your friend, Juice? I chuckled.

She scrunched up her face. "No! Never. I want a man with his name on a credit card, not his arm. Not to say I'm looking for a man with money, but I'm thirty-two. I want a stable man that I can depend on mentally, spiritually, and physically. A man sta-ble within himself and his career. I want a solid relationship, not just a night on the town and hot sex. That's not me. I hope I'm not scaring you off but I want a child and family. My ex-husband didn't want any children of his own. He just wanted to sleep with them."

Her last statement surprised me. "What do you mean?

"No, he wasn't a child molester, but he liked them young, between eighteen and twenty-one. I'm sorry, I'm rambling. Let me explain this to you. My ex was thirty. When I met him, I was eighteen. I was impressed by the nice cars and money he kept throwing at me. He bought me everything I wanted. He took me everywhere. I didn't fall in love with him; I fell in love with the lifestyle he was giving me but I wanted to be more than the woman on the side. He left his wife and we got married six months after his divorce was finalized. He owned an electrical contracting firm. His father had started it, so money was not a problem. The first three years I was in a fantasy. Then, it was after my twenty-second birthday that he lost interest in me. I got too old for him. I caught him cheating three times in the next two years. He had me believing I was stupid and if I left him that I would never be able to make it on my own. I had my looks but they would only take me so far. So that's when I started saving my money. He wasn't giving me much any more. He would give me enough to take care of the house and that was it. He would buy my clothes and pay for my trips to the beauty salon but as far as any extra money, that wasn't happening. He also told me that if I left him I wouldn't get a dime. He had the money to hire the best lawyer. So I came up with a plan: every night

I took twenty dollars from his wallet. He never kept track of his money, anyway. So for three years, the twenty dollars a day and the money I saved from cutting coupons came up to $23,000. I rented a room and went to Long Island Beauty School and when I graduated, I opened up my salon. It wasn't much, but now I just lease the storefront next door and I'm expanding. So that's where I stand now."

I could tell her statement brought back bad memories for her and I felt sorry for asking. She tried to amass a smile, but it crumbled and she ended up looking down at the table. She tried to wipe the tears from her eyes but had ground her napkin to dust so I proceeded to wipe the tears and kiss her gently on the cheek.

Nino and Maria set our table. It was enough food to feed a small army and it smelled so good. "Dig in," he said, as he and Maria stood back like proud parents, I took a shrimp, tasted it and give him the thumbs up. Maria pulled him away to give us some privacy.

Trying to change the mood a bit I asked:

"So, Leslie, you did mention a twin. What's she doing?"

"Well, Lisa, is… let me put it like this: she's living off her body. No, that doesn't sound right. She dances in videos. She's been doing it for the past ten years and she makes good money but at her age, she doesn't get as much work as she used to. She's an old lady in a young girl business. I know thirty-two isn't old but to retire at thirty-two is great if you're a millionaire and she's far from that. Leslie bit into a shrimp.

"Well, what about you, Mr. Miller? Tell me about yourself."

I thought for a few seconds. Should I tell her the truth? No, not all of it.

"Darius, D-a-r-i-u-s," Leslie repeated. She giggled at my hesitation

"Well, I grew up in Rosedale. I have three sisters."

"How about the little girl who called me a hoe." Leslie asked with a smile.

"Well, let me start from the beginning. First there is my sister Elaine and her daughter, Shana. She's the one who called you a hoe. Then there's Joyce, then me, and my youngest sister, Janet, and her son who wants to be a wrestler; and my son Darius Junior, who everyone calls DJ. Other than that, I also have a son from my first marriage."

"First marriage," Leslie repeated. "How many times were you married?" Her facial expression was a mix between surprise and concern.

"Only once. Maybe I worded it wrong. I was married young and it only lasted one year.

Now she had a look of interest.

"What happened, if you don't mind me asking?"

"Not at all. Well, we were both young and had been together since we were kids. It's what everyone expected and we spent a

34

lot of money on it. There were about forty-five people in the wedding party alone. We made a very big deal about it but my heart was not in it. I was really in love with someone else but I married this girl just to please everyone else and after we married, I didn't want to be tied down. I know I was wrong but I wasn't ready. So it was best we split up because I was making both of us miserable. She had gotten pregnant right before we got married so my son was born in early March and we separated that same August. His name is Darian. He spends summers and either Christmas or Thanksgiving with me, so I try to maintain some balance in his life. Other than that, I work six to seven days a week, ten to twelve hours a day, unless I have DJ for the weekend."

Nino walked back to the table and handed me the bill. He then looked over to Leslie and smiled.

"If only I was twenty years younger." He started to clear the table as Leslie grabbed the bill.

"Let me pay for this. You spent enough money tonight, so let me pay for this."

She looked at the total and her eyes nearly jumped out of her head.

I snatched the bill back. "I asked you out. Tonight is on me, so don't worry about the bill." The bill was for a $235 dollars. I counted out cash and then added an extra twenty for the tip. Leslie offered to pay the tip, but I turned her down. Nino finished clearing the table and went into the back.

"So Leslie, it's getting late and as much as I don't want this night to end, they're going to close on us."

Her cell phone rang and before she had a chance to respond, she held up a finger to indicate that it would only be a minute. I could read the surprised expression on her face and then hear it in her voice. It was Juice. I excused myself from the table because I had gotten pissed just that quick. A damn good night ruined. I was glad I held myself back. I had been hurt real bad before and I didn't really trust women. By the time I got to the back. Nino and Maria were smiling again. I hugged Nino and then kissed Maria and told her she wasn't too old and if she ever wanted to leave Nino, to call me. That brought a wide grin to her face. She gave me a bear hug. "Okay, okay" Nino said as he handed me back the $235.00 for the bill.

"Darius, she is beautiful, try to settle down with this one." I shook his hand and walked back to the table, where Leslie sat waiting.

"I'm sorry Darius. That was Juice. The contractor who is doing the work on my shop is a friend of his and Juice thinks because his friend is helping me, that we're friends. I'm sorry."

"Oh please. No need to explain, Leslie."

"Darius, please. I had a wonderful night. How about I treat you tomorrow, if I'm not being too forward? I want to see you again."

I smiled.

Chapter 6

Walking into the lobby of my building, my thoughts of Leslie were shattered. My third floor tenant was sleeping on the steps with her head on her lap.

"Tracy, Tracy, wake up." I tapped her gently. She looked up at me with her big, beautiful brown eyes. Tracy was twenty-one and about 5'6". She had a mocha brown complexion and her hair was always braided. She was stunning; I mean, wow! She was built like a goddess but you wouldn't know it because she always wore those over sized sweat suits.

"Tracy, your mother's at it again? All she could do was nod her head. Tracy's Mom was an HIV-positive crack head who would suck and fuck anyone to get high and when she had a man up-stairs with a little money, she would throw Tracy out because she did not want Tracy drawing attention away from her. I offered

Tracy an apartment but she turned it down. She had to watch her little brother all the time. He would sleep through his mother's late night sexual endeavors but the next morning, Tracy made sure he had a good meal and was ready for school before she got to school herself. Through all the bullshit she dealt with she was still able to maintain a 4.0 grade average at Columbia University.

"Tracey, you have my spare key, why don't you use it? What are you doing out here?"

"Darius." She hugged me and started crying. "I'm sorry if I caused you trouble when I went in.

DJ's mom was there and she called me a crack head slut and said I was just like my mother. Darius, "I'm sorry."

The anger rose up in me within seconds. What the hell was Brenda doing in my apartment, and who does she think she is? How did that bitch get a key?

"Tracy, don't worry." I tried not to get so angry as to explode at the mere thought of Brenda invading my privacy. "Go down to my office in the basement and relax while I take care of this."

I strode into the apartment, livid. I found Brenda lying on my bed, wearing a bathrobe.

"Brenda, what the fuck are you doing in my apartment?!" The robe fell open enough for me to see that she had shaved her pubic hairs to resemble a heart.

God what did I ever see in this woman? She didn't even have enough ass to keep her pussy off the sheets.

"Darius, I wanted to surprise you. Please, have a seat and talk to me."

"Brenda, get up and get dressed now please! Because it isn't happening. Not now, not ever again."

"Darius, just stop. You know you want me." She reached for my zipper and had me out and in her mouth within seconds. I stepped back, tucked in, and rezipped my pants.

That took a lot of will power, but I was just that infuriated.

"No, Brenda! It's over. Get your shit and get the fuck out and wherever you got that key, put it back. If I catch you in my apartment again, I'll have you arrested."

"But Darius..." Before she could get the words out, I had the front door open and threw her clothes out in the hallway.

Taken aback, Brenda quickly jumped off the bed. "Darius let me get dressed!" I pushed her out and snatched my robe off her. Brenda stood there, butt-naked in the hall, crying. I felt sorry for her but didn't give in and slammed the door in her face. I couldn't allow these things to happen. I wouldn't look at her but I had to give her back her shoes. I opened the door slightly and slid her pumps out. I looked her in the face and closed the door quickly. I knew she still loved me but where there was love, there was sometimes pain. I didn't want her in that way and I hoped she understood.

Determined not to go outside to see my baby's mother, I called downstairs to check on Tracy. She picked up on the first ring.

"Tracy, lock the basement door and come up here. I pulled the couch out for you and there's a blanket and pillow. Lock the door when you get in."

Chapter 7

I woke up to the smell of bacon and God knows I love me some bacon. When I walked into the kitchen Tracy had breakfast done. She had brought her little brother Marcus down. He looked just like Tracy with those big eyes, except his were hazel. With a mouth full of pancakes he yelled out, "Hi Dary!" They were both so beautiful, how could their mother treat them the way she did? Tracy was wearing her trademark oversized sweatpants but unlike before she had on a sports bra. It's the first time I saw her underdressed like that. She had her belly button pierced and it looked great. Matter of fact, she looked great.

"I hope you don't mind that I cooked breakfast. I cooked everything you like."

I had to admit that Tracy was a damn good cook.

"You know I don't mind, Tracy," I replied. I guess I was staring too hard because she pulled on an oversized T-shirt.

"Tracy, do you mind staying down here today? I need someone to watch DJ."

Marcus yelled, "Oh, please, please, let's stay! I want to play with Deejay.

"I'll have my sister drop him off around noon, and don't let her talk you into watching the other brats."

"No problem, Darius. I think I'll take them to the park."

Breakfast was great but I was late. I just had enough time to sample a few pancakes and load a handful of bacon onto a paper towel.

The day was going great except for the few times the image of Brenda standing naked in my hallway, crying, came to mind. When I got to the office, I was surprised to find Leslie had flowers delivered to me, thanking me for last night and asking me to stop by the shop if I was in the area. Shit, I could have been in Iraq and I would have stopped by, saying I was in the area.

My good mood changed when I pulled up in front of the Salon and saw Juice's 750 parked out in front. I started to pull off but thought, "Hell, why should I run away?" I wanted to know what was really up with Juice.

I walked into the shop and the receptionist jumped up right away.

"Mr. Miller, how are you doing?" She started to sweat.

The place was packed and it seemed like every head in there turned to look at me. I felt embarrassed.

"My name is April, nice to meet you. Leslie is next door with the contractor. She couldn't stop talking about the wonderful time she had last night."

Well, that explained the looks from everyone but it didn't explain Juice. April led me next door and the first thing I saw was Juice sitting on a table, while Leslie was talking to the contractor, whom I recognized. Juice looked at April and gave her a look that said there wasn't much love between them. I swear I heard April call him a punk bitch under her breath.

"Darius, I love the motto on your truck. It's a little crass but it's great." April smiled, trying to divert her attention from Juice.

April was an attractive brown skinned woman with great legs in her miniskirt, but the gold tooth ruined what she had going for her. I used to think my motto was offensive but people love it and it helps them to remember the company name better.

Juice said something inaudible. April looked at him and called him a punk bitch again, this time louder. She turned back to me. "Nice to have met you, Darius." And walked out the door.

Just then Juice walked over and extended his hand. "Derrick, right? No, it's Darius. I'm sorry."

He must have loved those tank tops. Today he wore a black one with a gold chain. This time I noticed he had a jail physique: well-formed upper body but no legs.

43

"Well, Darius, I thought you'd be out making money for your boss."

"No, Juice, my boss gives me ten minutes for lunch."

I hate using the "n" word but I could buy this wanna-be baller with the spare change under my couch cushions. I had nothing positive to say to this brother. I walked over to Leslie and tapped her on the elbow. She turned and said, "Hi, babe. I want you to meet the contractor."

Before she could say his name I said, "Paulie, how are you?"

Paul F. Mingo was close to fifty but was in damn good shape. What made me jealous was that he never worked out and ate like a horse, but was strong as an ox for his age. If it weren't for the few gray hairs in his beard, you would have sworn he was in his mid-thirties. To remedy that, he kept his head and face clean-shaven.

"What up, Big D? You know I'm alright. You know this beautiful lady right here?"

"Yes, I do, Paulie. Not as well as I hope to, though."

Leslie smacked my arm. "Okay, let's keep this rated PG."

I bent down and kissed her on the cheek. "Anything you want. So Paulie, what's it look like, much work?"

"No, it's not that bad, mostly cosmetic change. I can have everything done in two weeks."

Paulie was a good worker. If he said he would have something done in two weeks, it would be done in a week and a half. All his workers were ex-cons. The name of his company was R.A.F. Construction. It stood for Ready and Available Felons, but if you asked Paulie, he'd say it stood for Ralph A. French, some mystery owner.

"Hey, Darius. Why don't you do the plumbing for your friend? You could save her some money."

Damn Paulie, you just put me on the spot. I usually don't do work for family or friends because if you don't charge, you lose, and if you do charge, they usually don't pay you much.

"Alright Paulie, no problem." I grinned tightly, glaring at him.

Leslie squeezed my hand. "You sure you don't mind, Darius? I will pay you." The sweet look in her eyes damn near made my heart melt.

"No problem. It's no problem at all. I'll do it at night." She kissed me on the cheek and I felt my heart dance.

"Paulie, how do you know Juice?"

"D, that was in another life. Okay, Ms. Leslie, I will get back to you Monday morning with the estimates and D and I will send you a copy of the plans. And since you are a friend of Big D here, I'll throw in an extra 10% discount."

As we walked towards the door Juice joined us outside. Paulie gave Juice a very cold handshake before he walked over to me and gave me a brotherly hug. "I'll call you Monday," he said and walked off. We stood on the sidewalk for a few seconds.

"Leslie, I'll call you later." Juice said. He went to kiss her but she backed off.

"Thank you, Juice, for all your help"

His eyes searched around. He must have felt hurt because he just turned around and walked off toward his car. For a brief second I felt sorry for him. I turned to Leslie. "Thanks for the flowers. It was a first. I never received flowers from a woman before." I knew she had been thinking of me and that was better than any gift she could have given me. I glanced over and saw Juice was talking to a heavyset brother that I also knew. The other guy pulled something out his jacket pocket.

Juice called me over. "Yo Darius, come over please."
When Leslie and I got to this car, I noticed two Rolex watches. The salesman, Steele, was telling Juice he just bought them . He even produced the receipt from the Visa cards. Steele was a large brother, about 6'2" and 290 lbs., with a voice that sounded like he woke up every morning and gargled with hot gravel and broken glass.

"Look, my man." Steele said. "Check out the warranty for both of them. It's the best deal you'll every get. One watch costs $4,000 but I'll give you both for $3,000."

All the paperwork looked legit. I examined the watches closely and looked at Juice. "It's a bargain," I said with a straight face.

"Then why don't you buy one?" He challenged.

"Well, Juice, it's a little too expensive for me but a brother like you should have no problem."

"These are real?" Leslie asked Steele.

"Of course, Miss, you can't beat a Rolex."

"They are very nice," she agreed.

That was all Juice needed to hear." I'll take one," he said proudly. "I'll only give you a grand." He and Steele went back and forth until they settled on $1,100.

Juice pulled a knot of money from his front pocket, counted off $1,100, and handed it over to Steele. Steele gave him the watch, case, and all the paperwork. Juice was very proud of himself. He jumped in his car with a big smile and pulled off quickly.

"What's up, baby?" I said, I gave Steele a quick hug and Leslie looked surprised.

"You two know each other?"

"Yeah. Steele and I go way back. He's come a long way from selling fake VCRs and camcorders."

Leslie cocked her head in confusion.

"Steele's a con man," I explained. He'd sell anything from the Brooklyn Bridge to the Empire State Building.

She turned to him. "You mean to tell me that those watches were fake? What about the Visa card number and the receipt?"

Steele laughed.

"Show her, Steele." I urged.

He pulled out three more watches, each with a receipt and warranties. Everything looked legit. The only way to know the watches were not real was for a jeweler to appraise them. If the jeweler wasn't good he could be fooled as well. All of the watches had the same serial number.

"You can buy the watch and receipt for about $150.00 each," Steele explained.

Leslie just shook her head. As for me, I felt great. I loved to see a hustler get hustled.

Chapter 8

Following Leslie into the salon, I couldn't tell what kind of jeans she was wearing but she was definitely working them. I almost didn't hear April say hello again. Once more, all eyes seemed to be on me. The place was still packed; at least twenty different people were being worked on in different phases of their beauty transformation. The place was bigger than I thought. Six beauticians worked in separate stations by the wall. The wall was mirrored and there was a small chandelier in the middle of the room that reflected light in the mirror. The back wall held six dryers with reclining chairs. Right next to the dryers was what was called the "Homey Hangout." There was a big screen TV with both a Play Station 2 and an Xbox hooked up to it. There were several game discs for them as well. The floor was cheap industrial tile but it was polished to a high gloss. It picked up the little sunlight coming through the window and bounced its shine to the mirror.

Leslie held my hand and introduced me to several beauticians and customers. I nodded my hellos and walked through the first door, where there were three stations set up for nails and pedicures. There were three women getting their nails done and five more waiting. I was introduced to more people before Leslie pulled me through the rear door that led to her small office. It held a metal and wood desk and the same tiled floor as the Homey Hangout but without the high gloss. There was a couch against one wall while the other held a table with a microwave and a small refrigerator. The last wall held racks of magazines, newspapers, and a photo album.

"Have a seat, Darius. I can't leave but I want us to have a picnic."

I sat on the couch and Leslie pulled a blanket from a small closet that I hadn't noticed and spread it on the floor. She went to the small refrigerator in the corner and removed sandwiches and soda.

"I know that this isn't as expensive as last night, but it's the best I could come up with in twenty minutes."

I sat on the floor as she set up the food next to me and pulled some plants close to us.

She sat the flowers I sent to her on the opposite side of us before she sat down across from me and smiled. "I hope you enjoy your lunch."

I really didn't give a damn about the food. I was just enjoying the fact that I was next to her. I leaned over to give her a kiss. She backed up. "If you want a kiss, there is one on the desk." I looked over to the desk and there was a jar of Hershey kisses. The shock must have registered on my face because Leslie leaned over and gave me a quick peck on the lips.

"Now eat," she commanded.

The Swiss and Turkey sandwiches were good and I helped her clean up and fold the blanket. I pulled some of the magazines off the shelf. She had Essence, Ebony, and Black Enterprise. The Black Enterprise was an old issue with Damon Dash and Jay-Z on the cover. "You read all of these, "I asked.

"No, not really. I get them for the customers. I'm not interested in that. I don't even read the newspaper, except for the horoscopes."

I was dumbstruck. "Leslie, I'm not trying to get into your business, but you should make good money from the shop. I think you should invest into it more."

She just shook her head. "No, I just put it in the bank."

"Okay, Leslie, let's change the subject. Politics. Do you get involved?"

She shook her head again. "No. There's no use. My vote doesn't mean anything."

"Then what do you do besides work here? What outside interest do you have?

51

"None. I work here, go home, and to the movies once in a while."

"What about church?" I asked.

"Nothing special," she replied.

It was sad to say, but instantly I lost some respect for her. There is nothing worse than a black person who doesn't use political power that our own people died for.

"Leslie, do the things going on around the world have any interest to you?"

"No, not really," she said.

Wow! I was dumbstruck. She has got to be kidding. It was mind blowing how sheltered she kept herself. At that point she was turning me off. I want intelligence with beauty. After sex, what the hell would we talk about? She was limited. There was a silence between us for a minute. I looked at my watch and realized I should be going.

"Leslie, I should be getting back to work."

She walked over and kissed me. I must say I gave in because after the passionate kiss, I came up for air and forgot all about the awkward conversation and kissed her again, and it was a toe-curling, penis-rising kiss. I know Leslie felt my erection but she just grabbed me tighter and pulled me closer.

My hand caressed her ample posterior and lifted her up a bit. My only thoughts were to get her to the couch. I spun slightly to the right and to the couch. We both fell back onto it. My tongue went from her mouth to her ear to her neck and to her collarbone.

She had on a T-shirt and my hands were up under it, raising it up. I kissed the top of her breast and her breathing stalled. She let it out slow and steady.

I reached around with my right hand to unfasten her bra. Damn, it fastened in the front. Fuck it. I just pulled them out from the top. I devoured the nipples one at a time before I finally opened the bra and released them totally. I pulled my head back and got a good look. Her nipples were rock hard. I took the right one in my mouth while I played with the left. With my moistened left thumb and forefinger, I pushed them together and licked them from left to right and up and down.

"Stop, Darius! We can't do this yet, okay? I didn't stop and she didn't push me away. Her body relaxed more and I kissed my way down her belly to the top of her jeans then back up to her breasts. I had to test the waters so I opened her jeans and had my hands between her thighs. I noticed she was clean—shaven and her panties were damp. Shit, they were past damp; they were drenched. I rubbed her lower lips, parted them a bit then slid a finger in.

"Mmmm, no Darius." I kissed Leslie passionately. "No" was the last thing I wanted to hear. I worked another finger around then slid it in too. I rubbed her clitoris up and down and worked my fingers in vigorous motion, while massaging her breasts with my tongue. She tensed up and grabbed a pillow from the couch and put it over her face.

Her breathing kept getting deeper and deeper. Moans of pleasure escaped from behind the pillow.

"Darius, Darius, Darius…OH God, Darius!" Leslie pulled the pillow tighter to her face, let out a scream and arched her body up. I hooked my fingers, got deep inside and slowly stroked in and out. I pulled her jeans and panties down to her ankles, opened her legs wide, and worked those two fingers with precision while I went back to tongue massage her breasts. I heard what sounded like a whimper then a soft cry, then a loud moan or low scream into the pillow. Leslie arched her body upward again and quaked with what seemed like a mini-explosion over my hand. She tensed up again and fell back onto the couch. I kissed her for a few seconds but she pushed me away, got up and walked over to a small closet. She grabbed a towel and threw me one also.

"That wasn't supposed to happen. Please leave now." She said with a stern face.

I didn't know what to say. I walked over to her. "Leslie, please talk to me."

"No. Leave, Darius," she repeated. I pulled her to me and she started crying.

"That wasn't supposed to happen, Darius. I'm not a slut. It's been a long time and I lost my head. I got caught up in the moment." She fell into me. "Darius, I don't want you getting the wrong ideas."

"Listen, Leslie, we are adults. If anything happens, it's because we both wanted it to happen. So don't feel any way because I won't lose respect for you." I kissed her and she tasted salty from tears.

"Thank you, Darius. I feel better. I want this to be the beginning of a relationship and not just some fling."

"Leslie, I feel the same way."

"Leslie?" A voice came from the other side of the door.

"Yes, April?"

"Leslie, Mrs. Austin insists on speaking with you before she leaves."

"Tell her I'll be out in few minutes." She looked up at me. "Thank you Darius for understanding."

Leslie kissed me again but this time it was not so salty.

We walked to the front, where she paused and told Mrs. Austin that she would be with her in one minute, and walked me outside to my truck. She kissed me once more and asked," Can I see you again later?"

"I don't think so, I said. I saw her face change rapidly. "It's not what you think. I have DJ for the weekend. So I must be with him tonight, unless you want to come over and help me chase a four year old around the house."

She gave me another hug and kiss. "I don't mind at all."

I watched her turn and walk away. Damn, what was I doing? I usually don't bring women around my son. I don't want him getting attached to anyone because most of them I didn't plan on being around to long. I thought about what just happened in her office. I could tell she wasn't lying about not being with anyone in a long time. When she came, it felt like someone opened a fire hydrant and the size of the wet spot on the couch covered almost two cushions.

Chapter 9

"Daddy, the door!"

"I'll get it, DJ"

"No, I'll get it."

DJ is only four but her acts fourteen. He loves to answer the phone, which I don't mind but the door is something different.

"Daddy, I can get it."

I gave him one of those looks that parents hand down from generation to generation that lets a child know there will be no discussion and that the answer is no. He stopped dead in his tracks and turned slowly, looking sad, but it wasn't working. He looked so much like my mother it was crazy. He has her light yellow complexion, thick, jet-black curly hair and eyebrows with bright brown eyes, but his dimples came from my father and me. I pointed him to the bedroom but he didn't respond. I opened the front door and the light in the hallway seemed to illuminate Leslie with a glow that was reminiscent of an angel. DJ and I both stared at her beauty until she said," Darius, I have another bag in my car." I didn't notice the two plastic grocery bags by her feet.

"What is this? You didn't have to bring anything."

"I never go to anyone's home without anything. Plus, I brought something for DJ.

DJ's eyes quickly perked up. "For me?

"Yes," Leslie smiled.

He was out the door so fast; all I saw was a blur. He got to the vestibule door and looked back at me impatiently. I sat the two bags inside the door and walked out. I let Leslie walk first so I could get a good look. She wore a pair of beige Capri pants, brown sandals and what looked to be some lightweight tank top the same shade as her sandals. The Capri accented her assets to perfection. I had to untuck my T-shirt to hide the fact I was hard enough to cut diamonds.

Leslie turned off the alarm on her Jaguar XJP convertible, which was blue with beige seats and chromed out factory rims. What more does a man want? A beautiful woman with a beautiful car. Only thing I needed now was for the New York Knicks to win the championship and I'd be a very happy man. Inside the car was another grocery bag and a truck for DJ. He tried to grab the box but it was too large. He looked up at me with a hurt look. I wanted to get a better look at the car but DJ was rushing me. He wanted to get his hands on the truck. Leslie grabbed the bag and closed the door. I glanced up and my second floor tenant Mr. James was giving me the thumps-up sign. I nodded my head in return, which was the universal sign for what's up.

"Darius, just let me know where you keep the pots and pans, and spices, and you can help DJ with the truck."

"DJ is a big boy he doesn't need the help, Let me give you a tour of my apartment. It's not that big, but its home.

My living room was a Jennifer Convertibles special. I'm not much on decorating. Hunter green leather sofa with matching love seat, lounge chair and ottoman. The glass coffee table held more magazines and books than it ever held coffee. It all sat on an imitation Oriental rug, black border with green, white and a touch of red. I could have afforded the real thing but it matched everything else. Plus, I got it from one of my customers who owned a carpet store. I also had what no man should live without: a 53"flat screen TV. I have every channel known to man on an illegal box. For entertainment I have Xbox, Play stations 1 and 2, Dreamcast and Sega Genesis. For the old school nights, I have the original Atari. I know it's a classic, but I still love playing Space Invaders and Pac Man.

Leslie looked around. "This place needs a female touch. Some cute curtains and a few pictures."

I smiled nervously, "yeah, maybe you're right." Hell no, she was dead wrong. I wasn't about to tell her that the last woman that came over on a regular basis started giving my place a "female touch." She had about five pictures of herself, combs, toothbrushes, panties and bras. I knew I had to let her go when I found used tampons in the bathroom wastebasket.

Next was the bedroom. Nothing special. A king-sized bed with brass and cherry foot-and headboards. The dresser is also hand-made cherry wood with a matching chest and nightstands, which held crystal lamps. I got those as a wedding present almost twelve years ago. The light beige carpet had three pads underneath. It was so soft that sometimes I slept on the floor. Leslie removed her sandals before she walked in. I was impressed. I usually had to remind people to take their shoes off. She went straight over to a black-and-white picture I had hanging of my "posse": Shana, my niece; Michael and Darius Junior, in a group hug.

"Darius, they are so cute! Are they your niece and nephew? They are adorable!"

"I know. That's the picture I look at every night before I go to sleep." She looked around some more and said, "This is very nice. It looks so expensive." If she only knew; everything I got was from my customers for almost nothing.

"Darius, everything looks great but let me start cooking and you can help DJ with the truck"

Believe me, DJ doesn't need help." I grabbed her and gave her a quick kiss. It felt so good that I picked her up on and carried her to the bed. I sat down with her on my lap.

"Darius, what are you doing?"

"Nothing. Let's just talk."

Leslie adjusted her body and put her arms around me. She kissed me hard and very passionately. "Now, what do you want to talk about?"

"Let's talk about the first thing that comes up." I winked.

Leslie smiled and jumped up. "No! You must be crazy. DJ is in the next room and the door is open." She caught on quick because I was the one who was up. She pulled me up and gave me a kiss. "Now, let me cook and that 'thing" that came up, we'll talk about it later."

Dinner was okay but nothing spectacular. Leslie needed to learn how to season her food but I could work with her. You can't spend your whole life looking for the right person. You have to become or build that person and Leslie had one hell of a foundation to start with.

"Daddy, can we go outside and play with my truck?" DJ asked.

"Did you read all the instructions?"

"Yes, Dad," DJ replied. He had a smile on his face that would melt the coldest heart. His dimples were deep enough to swim in.

"Okay, DJ, only for half an hour." He was gone, leaving another blur.

Leslie looked at me with a confused look on her face. "I thought he was only four?"

"He is," I answered, knowing where this was going.

She shook her head. "And he read the instructions?"

"Yes," I smiled. "DJ, come here for a minute."

"Daddy, I'm ready." He was at the kitchen doorway with the truck and remote control in his hands.

"DJ, what's the capital of New York?" I questioned.

"That's easy. Albany."

"Okay. What's the capital of Colombia?

"That's easy too. Bogotá.

"Okay, DJ grab the newspaper and read the first article." He opened the paper and read the article with little hesitation and only needed help with one word.

"Okay. Good. One more thing and we can go out. What is white America most afraid of?"

"An educated black man. They would rather see a black man play basketball or in concert, but not sitting across from them at their dinner table dating their daughter. That's why I will never sell drugs and destroy my people. I want to see them educated and to prosper."

He stood there, proud; because he knew what he had said was right. The look on Leslie's face was pure shock. She walked to DJ and hugged him. He laid his head on her breasts, smiling. Smart kid. He's a breast man like his father.

"Okay, DJ, let's go outside before it gets dark."

Leslie and I sat on the stoop while DJ played with his truck between two imaginary boards. He couldn't go past the building on either side.

"So, how was dinner," she asked.

I usually don't like to lie because I suffer from CRS (Can't Remember Shit) Syndrome.

"It was good," I said as enthusiastically as I could. She didn't notice that I couldn't look her in the eye.

She just smiled. "I'm trying, but I don't cook much."

"So Leslie, where do you plan on being in the next five years?"

She looked up in the air as if God were going to give her the answer, then back at me. She blinked and said, "Darius, I really don't know. I live my life day by day. I never think that far in advance. Maybe I should because DJ had me thinking. What he said was very deep. I barely graduated from high school and I wasn't interested in college. I feel lost when the conversation in the shop turns to politics. A lot of times, I don't even get involved with what is said because I'm not smart enough to understand." She leaned back and slumped down, turned her head and wiped her tears.

"Look, DJ is only four and he's smarter than me. I know he learned all that from you. So I don't think you would be interested in someone as stupid as me."

I took her hand in mine and pulled her closer to me. "Leslie, you are far from being stupid. You may not think that you are able to follow the conversations in the shop, but you own the shop. So who's the intelligent one? You are financially independent, you own your own home and a very nice car, and you're expanding. You have a lot going for yourself. If you want to be more socially conscious, I can help you. I'll give you books to read and the newspaper is a good start, but you can't believe every thing they say. A woman who has achieved what you have is an intelligent woman." I said confidently

"Darius, you don't understand. I went to Long Island Beauty School but I failed the state board exam five times. I feel like I can't even achieve my dreams."

"Leslie, when is the next time you can take the test?"

"Why, Darius? I'm not taking the test!" She yelled and waved her arms. DJ turned around and questioned me with his look. I nodded my head. "Its okay, DJ." He turned back around and began playing with his truck again.

"Leslie, I can help you study for the test and I can guarantee you will pass. Let me see your study books, and there should be a test prep book. I'll pick it up Monday and we'll begin Monday night." I was not sure if I wanted to put myself through that again. "Please, Leslie just give it a chance. I have faith in you; have faith in yourself, please."

"Thank you, Darius. I don't know what to say. It's like I've known you for years. I feel so comfortable in your arms. You've been on my mind all day and night. You are so different from most of the men I've dated lately; they only talk about what they can do to me or what they can do for me. You treat me with respect and I felt you were a special person the day I met you in the gym. You confirmed that last night. What happened today made me feel so embarrassed, but you gave me back my dignity instead of making me feel cheap. What I'm trying to say is, I may be crazy, but I'm developing strong feelings for you already." She turned and looked me in the eye. "Don't hurt me, please." She then kissed me gently on the cheek and laid her head on my chest and squeezed me tight. She was putting herself in my hands and letting me mold her mind. I could create what I want; build the perfect person for me.

"Okay, Darius. What do you want in the next five years?" She looked at me suddenly. Damn, I wasn't ready to answer that question. I wanted information; I wasn't ready to give any out. Should I tell her the truth yet?

"Well, let me see. I want health and happiness. I want to be a better father to my sons. I want to help my community and people more."

"Darius, that sounds good."

It was mid-July but a cool chill had fallen over us. "Wow," I said. "I just got cold all of a sudden?"

The wind picked up and the leaves were waving in the breeze. The sound of thunder could be heard in the distance. I didn't know if it was luck or divine intervention but rain was coming down and I was off the hook. Just then the sky opened up and the rain poured by the bucket load. The three of us were soaked to the bone by the time we got inside. I got us towels to dry off with.

"DJ, take off your clothes and get ready for a bath"

65

"Dad, the rain cleaned me off. I don't need a bath, I'll take one tomorrow."

Sometimes I can't believe this is my kid. I take three showers a day and I love the feel of hot water against my skin.

"Okay, put on dry underwear, and get ready for bed, but I want you to study for at least half an hour and then you can watch TV in my room."

"Yes, sir." He said while running off.

I turned to Leslie, who had the towel wrapped around her, shaking.

"I'm sorry. Let me get you something dry to put on. Take the towel and get out of those wet clothes. You know where the bathroom is. I'll be there in a minute."

I went to my bedroom and saw DJ jumping on my bed in his underwear, watching his favorite cartoon 'Dexter's Laboratory.' I gave him a look and he sat right down. I found a pair of sweatpants and a T-shirt for Leslie and another set for me, plus some socks. My feet were freezing.

I knocked on the door. "Leslie, I'm going to turn my head so you can take these sweats." I opened the door and she had her back to me. She had the towel still wrapped around her but I could see the bottom of her butt checks sticking out from under the towel. I got so hard it hurt. What little I saw was so sexy I almost lost it. I dropped the clothes on the floor and closed the door. I was changed and on the couch by the time she came out. I hung my wet clothes on the shower door.

"If you don't mind, can I wear these home? I'll wash them and bring them back tomorrow."

"Sure, no problem, Leslie. So let's talk about the shop. What type of renovations are you doing?"

"Well, I'm just expanding to accommodate more beauticians. I rent booths for one hundred and seventy-five dollars a week.

If I add six more booths and two more nail stations, I should be okay. The only problem is keeping the booths rented to beauticians with a good enough flow so they can pay the weekly rent."

"Do you mind if I make a suggestion? Why don't you add a massage table and a small steam room? When I think of Total Experience Salon, I would like to think of being pampered from head to toe. Make it like a total day salon. Start with a steam room massage, and then a facial, eyebrow or bikini wax, pedicure and manicure; then send them next door to get their hair done. Make it a day retreat; a mini-vacation from a hard week at work. Serve light sandwiches, wine, cheese, and maybe a little champagne. Make it very elegant. Marble floors, chandeliers, plus paint the walls a soft pink. It's supposed to be a relaxing color. Tint the front window so that it is totally private and the only way to get in is from the existing salon. Also have it "appointment only" to give it that exclusive feel. You can charge about $125 and just pamper the hell out of them. Make it to the point that they don't want to leave." Damn I shocked myself about how much thought I put into her salon.

Leslie looked at me with confusion and maybe a hint of shock.

"I mean Damn, Darius! That sounds great- but wouldn't putting in a steam room be expensive?"

"No. I can do that for you. All you have to do is buy the supplies."

"Really? But what about Paulie? How much extra would it cost?"

"Leslie, it takes money to make money. All you have to do is say you want it done, and I'll talk to Paulie."

"Darius, it all sounds great, but I'm not sure".

"Listen, Leslie, that's the problem with black people. They're scared to take risks when it comes to entrepreneurship. Advertise. I can't see any way you can fail. Women spend almost $150 to get their hair braided, and I'm talking about their whole bodies. It's something you don't see much in our community. It's a total relaxation center. You can offer aromatherapy and the right music."

"Darius, how would I market this?"

"Leslie, any women's magazine, local newspaper, radio station, or cable. My company runs ads on cable all the time. Transit authority offers special rates for buses. They even offer deals for routes. Trust me and give it a shot. I'll help you any way I can."

"Darius, I'm giving you my heart and my trust. Don't hurt me."

She came in close and whispered.

I leaned back on the couch; my molding process was beginning and the subject was willing.

Just then I heard a crash.

"What was that?" The noise came from the bedroom. "What is DJ doing?" I jumped up to investigate and Leslie was right on my heels. DJ was asleep. In fact, he was snoring. He must have fallen asleep with the remote in his hand because it was on the floor and the batteries were against the wall. DJ was hanging halfway off the bed. Before I reached him, Leslie was picking him up and moving him to the center of the bed. She put the blanket over him and whispered, "Good night." Good maternal instincts, another plus for her. I may be able to turn her into the person I've always wanted. I picked the remote and batteries up and turned off the TV. We walked out and closed the door. Before we got to the couch, I spun her around and kissed her. I reached my hand into her sweat pants and picked her up. She wrapped her legs around my waist and her arms around my neck, and returned the kiss with equal passion. I slid the sweat pants down as much as possible and walked her over to the couch, but that was a bad move because the damn leather couch was cold; it was always cold.

"No, Darius, not now. We can't do this," Leslie said in between kisses. "The couch is cold." She pushed me off her and pulled her pants back up.

"Darius, I don't know what you did to me but I can't trust myself around you. What the hell did you do to me this afternoon? I have never come like that before in my life. My leg was shaking for an hour after you left. I had to take the pillows home and wash them. I'm almost scared of you."

"Nothing much. Just something I read about." I had an idea that would blow her mind if only she would let me. "Leslie I'll tell you what I did, only if you trust me. No sex. Just a massage."

"Darius, first tell me what you did."

"Okay. I'll tell you what I did only if you let me give you a massage. I need you to take your clothes off."

"Darius, no. "I'm not having sex with you." Leslie reached down in my lap. I was hard and pulsating but it wasn't the sex I needed tonight. I needed her to trust me and let me work my magic so I would know that I had her hooked.

"Leslie, you said you trust me with your money and your heart. Now trust me with your body. If I do anything you don't like, just say stop and I will. Remember my son is in the next room and I'm raising him to be a man. If a woman says "No," then she means "No." So I'm asking you to trust me."

"I don't know why, but I'm going to trust you, Darius."

"Good. Stay here and get undressed while I get everything ready."

It took me ten minutes to get everything together and when I got back in the living room she was sitting on the couch, still dressed.

"Leslie, why are you still dressed?"

"Darius." She whined.

"Leslie, trust is the only way to have any kind of relationship. Trust. I'm not trying to make love to you. I just want to help you relieve some tension."

She pulled off her T-shirt and her breasts bounced. They were very firm. The nipples were hard and perfectly round. They had to be at least a 34D in high school. I used to love for girls to try to pass the pencil test. I would take a regular number two pencil and place it under their breasts to see if they were big enough to keep the pencil from falling. Leslie would have no problem passing that test. I could see that she was nervous.

I walked over and kissed her. "You look beautiful." Everything I needed was in a cardboard box.

First, the lights. I hit the dimmer and turned the lights down low. That set the mood. Now the perfect CD, Musiq Soul Child. The whole album was great from beginning to end. I then spread five comforters on top of each other. I wanted her to be comfortable. I put a little strawberry freshener in my humidifier. The whole place would smell like strawberries in a few minutes. Leslie was fidgeting. I hope she wouldn't change her mind.

"Lie down flat on your stomach." She didn't respond at first.

"Darius, I don't…what if DJ wakes up?"

"Leslie, he was up late last night and he was playing all day. I'll be lucky if he wakes up before noon tomorrow. Please relax, just lie down" She moved slowly to her knees and looked at me with pleading eyes. "Trust me."

She laid flat on her stomach. I gave her a pillow to put under her head. I started with the strawberry edible massage oil I'd heated up in the microwave. It was still good and hot. I poured it over her right shoulder and started to work it in, massaging from neck to shoulder. She was very tense.

"Leslie, please relax. It helps to listen to the music. Take slow breaths."

I poured the oil over her left shoulder and worked it in. I spread the oil down her back and massaged the muscles from her neck to her butt. At that point, she finally and completely let go. I pulled open the back of the sweatpants and poured oil over the left cheek, then the right, and worked it in. Leslie was moaning softly now.

I straddled her and noticed she was in a trance. I slowly licked down her spine, from the top of her neck to the top of her buttocks. The moans got louder. I removed the sweatpants and spread more oil down the right leg, over her foot, and then the left leg and foot. I massaged her toes and feet. I slowly placed tender kisses down her right leg and then up the left.

"Leslie, please turn over." She was so relaxed; it was as if she was in another world. She slowly turned over then adjusted the pillow and lay back with her legs open. She had shaved her pubic hairs and they were just starting to grow back. They weren't coarse but that was not the spot I needed yet, however, her lower lips looked so wet and kissable. The oil was still warm so I spread it all over her ample breasts, her flat, firm stomach, and down to her treasure chest. I worked the oil in slowly but firmly. I took my time on her breasts. I slowly stroked the nipples and Leslie started moaning again. I tasted the left nipple, then the right. She pushed by head down but I resisted. I would taste her, but not yet. I went to my box and pulled out two thermoses. I took an ice cube from one and rubbed it around her nipple. Her eyes opened with shock.

"Relax, baby." She closed her eyes and I finished icing her nipples. They got hard as marbles. I took the other thermos and drank from it; hot tea. I held a little in my mouth and sucked on her left nipple, then her right. The abrupt change in temperatures stimulated the nerve endings. Leslie lifted her head and opened her eyes, let out a loud moan, and said, "Oh, Darius." Then she closed her eyes again. I grabbed the warm oil and poured more around her nipples then massaged them in my hands. Her breathing started to get shallow and louder between the moans. I reached over and pulled out a very soft-bristled electric toothbrush out of my box of tricks. I hit the switch and turned it on. Leslie opened her eyes again, completely surprised.

"Please, baby. Close your eyes and trust me." She closed her eyes and I massaged her nipples with the toothbrush. Time for the taste test. Back to my box of tricks: extra strong mints. I popped two in my mouth, sucked them for a minute then chewed them. I spread her legs and blew my mint breath into her. She started to squirm but I grabbed her by the waist and went in and tasted her. My minty tongue probed her.

Leslie said, "No, Darius stop." At the same time she was trying to push my head inside her.

She opened her legs wide and I used my fingers to part her lower lips. I fondled her clitoris with my tongue and she went into a slight shake. I had her where I wanted her. I adjusted my position and rose up so I could massage her breasts with my tongue and let my finger take her home. I took two and inserted them as she screamed with pleasure. She removed the pillow from behind her head and covered her face to muffle the screams of ecstasy.

A lot of people know about a woman's G spot but in 1996, scientists were conducting an experiment to find a cure for vaginal dryness and discovered the "A" spot. I stuck my curved finger inside her vagina a third of the way up the front wall. Leslie was arching her back up and down and side to side trying to slide down on my finger. The moans were real loud, so I continued up until I felt a small spongy area that's the G spot. An amateur would have stopped there but I moved upward until I found her cervix. It feels like the tip of your nose. Then I felt around until I found her "A" spot. I lowered my fingers a fraction of inch and moved them in a clockwise motion over the spot. Leslie shook uncontrollably, raising her body up and down several times. Her body arched so high I thought her spine would snap. She let out what sounded like a primal scream. I licked my left hand and used it to tease her clitoris while the right worked its way from the A to G spot. She screamed again and shook like she was having a seizure. Her mouth was open like she wanted to scream, but nothing would come out. She started to mutter but I couldn't comprehend what she was trying to say. Then the floodgates opened and Leslie came. She had to have had back-to-back multiple orgasms because my hand was wet below my wrist. I removed my hand and watched the aftershocks. Her left leg was shaking out of control, the blankets were soaked and she turned on her side and hugged the pillow as she balled up in the fetal position. She was breathing hard and what she was trying to say I still didn't understand. It sounded like she was crying.

"Darius."

I finally recognized my name.

"Yes babe."

"Please lie down next to me and hold me." There were tears in her voice. I got another blanket, took off my clothes and lay down next to her and just held her.

Leslie turned and kissed me. "Darius, what did you just do to me? My leg is still shaking." She was still short of breath.

"Baby, just relax. I only want to make you happy any way I can."

She kissed my chest and we lay there until she fell asleep. I kissed her forehead; she was mine.

Chapter 10

The re-education of Leslie Ann Simmons.

That may sound far-fetched but I'm about to help her. There aren't many other guys who would help a woman unless they were in love or married. To use a word like "love" right now, for me, is just not happening; but I do have strong feelings for her. After stimulating her Saturday night, she stayed over and we spent all day Sunday together, plus DJ really likes her. We went to IHOP for breakfast then to the movies and spent the rest of the afternoon in the park, where she pushed DJ on the swing rode with him on the seesaw and chased him around the monkey bars. I have to admit that I really enjoyed myself. I was on my way to building that special person to spend the rest of my life with. The idea I came up with for the shop was getting me excited. I had it all planned like it was my business. I wanted Leslie to make it plus I wanted her to have her own money. Not like I was broke or cheap and couldn't afford to take care of her, but I've been hurt a time or two and was always careful that a woman wanted me for me and not my money. I worked too damn hard to get where I am now and was not about to lose it. She had to bring something to the table.

My cell phone began to ring.

"Atomic Sewer and Drain Cleaning. Darius Miller speaking. May I help you?

"Darius."

"Oh, not now, Brenda."

"Darius, how could you disrespect my mother's house like that?"

"Brenda, I didn't disrespect your mother's house. What are you talking about?"

"When you dropped DJ off, you had some woman in the car. I think that's real disrespectful. I would never bring another man to your mother's house."

All the pleasant thoughts of Leslie and our weekend together just zapped out of my head. Damn! I really didn't want to hear Brenda's shit so early on a Monday morning. I didn't even get in my office yet. Damn these cell phones.

"Darius, are you listening to me?"

I 'm stuck in traffic on the Cross Island Parkway. I think every-one in a square-mile radius can hear you. "Brenda, please."

"And when did you buy a new car? We need to talk. I need more money for DJ."

One, two, three, four, five. I took a deep breath, One, Two, Three, Four, and Five. Brenda was still running her mouth. I needed the time out before I said something I didn't mean.

"Brenda, stop for one minute. First of all, I parked down the block. So I didn't disrespect your mother's house. My friend took DJ out for the day and it was getting late, so I dropped him off and I didn't even pass your mother's house. I made a U-turn in the middle of the block." I was starting to get really pissed off. She knows how much money I'm worth and I worked out a very generous child support package. Someone else was behind this "I need more money" scam because no matter what, Brenda was a fair person even after I kicked her out naked. She would not have asked for extra.

"Darius, are you listening to me?"

"Brenda, if you don't like the amount I give you for DJ, take me to court. I guarantee you won't receive anything near what you get now. So, stop the bullshit and tell your mother to get a job and stop trying to use her grandson as a paycheck!" I shouted. I was really starting to get tense.

She stopped talking. She knew I was right.

"Brenda, please. I need to get to work. If you want, we can meet later this week and we can talk. We really need to so we can get a lot of these things over and done with so I can get on with my..."

"Darius."

"Bye, Brenda."

How could my weekend be so great and Monday get off to such a fucked-up start? Traffic began to flow once I got to the section where the Cross Island Parkway splits. Two lanes split left and became the Southern State Parkway going towards Eastern Long Island. The last right lane becomes the Belt Parkway heading towards Brooklyn and Staten Island.

Brenda's mother. The thought of her just seemed to consume my mind. The lady hated me the first moment she met me. I wasn't good enough for her daughter. In her eyes I was just a lowly plumber. She hated me when Brenda got pregnant and I wouldn't marry her. I would call the house to speak to Brenda and she would hang the phone up on me. It wasn't until DJ's first birthday at my house in Orange County that she realized that I had money and owned the company. What really made her cheap wig flip was that I had given a generous sum of money to charities that year. She's been trying to use DJ to get into my pockets ever since, and DJ has been spending a lot of time at her house.

"We need a pool, DJ needs to see his family, and I want to take him to see his relatives in Florida." She wanted to take DJ there. All she wanted was free trips and DJ was her excuse.

Well all this shit was about to come to an end because DJ is about to start hanging with Daddy a whole lot more and Grandma is going to get a job if she wants to travel.

My exit, Farmer's Blvd. My office is really an old gas station in the industrial section by Kennedy Airport. I got it when the big

79

Mobil station, three blocks down, opened up with the car wash and Kwik Mart. They just couldn't compete with the big boys so I got it real cheap. I took out all the repair bays but one and made a nice office for myself and a lounge for the guys with some weights, a TV and a soda machine, plus a few old sofas. Next to that was my dispatcher's office where my office manager, Valerie, worked. She liked to be called the office manager. I don't know why because the only people she managed were two part-time college students who answered the phone at night and on the weekends. Valerie's not there on nights and weekends to manage them but she wanted a title so she got one. Anything to keep my employees happy.

I pulled up in front of the building and a few of the guys waved, so I waved back and pulled old Patsy around back, where a Mercedes 320 coupe was blocking my usual spot. Shit! It couldn't be. First Brenda, now this. The personalized plates with "Ms. Drake" on it confirmed the fact that my day was getting fucked up fast. Before I was out of the car, Valerie was at the door. Valerie was in her late thirties and just had a newborn not to long ago. This morning anyone could tell that from the spot of baby vomit on her left shoulder.

"Mr. Miller, there is some white woman in your office who had me so pissed that I almost choked the shit out of her. She was demanding to be let in your office to wait for you. She said she would have me fired if I didn't treat her with the respect she deserved. I remembered her name from your appointment schedule and I knew you were trying to do business. So, I tried my hardest to be civil with her so I made her a cup of coffee. She had the nerve to tell me that the coffee tasted like mud. Mr. Miller, please take care of her before I catch a murder charge."

"Calm down, Valerie. I'll handle this. Why don't you transfer the phones to the answering service and go get yourself some breakfast, my treat. Go to the diner and take about an hour while I handle this." I handed her a twenty and knew there wasn't going to be any change because ever since her pregnancy, and even after, she's been eating like a horse. Valerie was very nice looking. I wouldn't say beautiful, but she had smooth dark brown skin, small narrow nose, slightly slanted eyes, full thick kissable lips, and she was full figured. She was 5'2", maybe 5'3". Since the baby she gained a lot of weight. The guys have been calling her "Shorty four by four" behind her back, meaning she was four feet tall and four feet wide; but nobody had the nerve to say it to her face.

I opened my office door and Marcia was sitting behind my desk.

"How did you get in my office? Didn't my office manager tell you to have a seat outside?"

Marcia just waved me off. "Darius, thank you for the flowers and the note. I knew you were smart and would come to your senses."

She was in my world and I didn't have to hold back. I walked over to my desk and extended my hand as to shake hers when she extended hers, I yanked her to her feet. She lost her footing and fell into me. I helped her stabilize her footing and pushed her away. Marcia was startled by my actions.

"What are you doing, Darius? You're hurting my wrist."

"I'm about to hurt your feelings too. Marcia, would you please step outside? I have things to take care of. When I'm ready to talk to you, I'll call you in."

"Mr. Miller, do you know who you're talking to?"

"Yes, Ms. Drake. I know damn well whom the hell I'm talking to. You can't just barge into my office like this, disrespecting my office manager. You don't own shit here and I don't care about you or your business. Just get the fuck out." The shade of red she turned didn't go well with the brown skirt suit she was wearing.

"You're right Darius, I'm sorry. I'll wait outside."

She went from red to light tan. She must have spent the week-end in the sun because she was tanned from head to toe. I could tell because the skirt she was wearing was cut high and the jacket with no blouse underneath was cut low showing her breasts were evenly tanned. I could damn near see her nipples and there was no bikini line. Even her hair was lighter. Her eyes shined brighter.

"Marcia, would you please step outside and have a seat." I repeated I will be with you in a few minutes."

Marcia walked out and closed the door. Damn, the bitch was going to cause problems. The way she got herself under control was scary. It's like she just flipped a switch and she was nice again. In a strange way, I was turned on. I walked over to my desk, sat down, leaned back and closed my eyes. I felt one hell of a headache coming on. I opened my eyes and scanned my desk. It needed to be cleaned. I had a stack of bills to pay on the right. Another stack of invoices to send out so I could get paid, on the left. The desk itself was dusty. The whole office needed to be cleaned. The bookshelf to the left had about an inch of dust. The carpet needed vacuuming. The small leather love seat was covered with boxes and T-shirts I'd just ordered with Atomic Sewer Cleaning: Satisfaction Guaranteed or Double Your Shit Back. Also some of my old shirts: The Real Turd Buster: Your Shit Is My Bread and Butter.

Damn, what was I going to do about Marcia? I would tell her I'm gay. No, that's not an option. I couldn't condemn myself like that. I'd cheated on every woman I was with and never got caught, but I couldn't do that now. I feel I have something special with Leslie and I'm not about to blow this chance I have with her. We all have strengths and weaknesses in this world and it is how we deal with them that determine our fate in this world. My weakness has always been beautiful women. I figured my fate was never to find someone special to settle down with. Fuck it. I marched to the door and opened it. "Ms. Drake,

83

please come inside." Marcia got up and walked into my office. I motioned for her to sit down in my chair.

"Please, Ms. Drake."

"Darius lets not be so formal."

"Okay, Marcia. This is how it's going to be. There is never going to be anything between us. I don't even want your business."

"Darius, you look great in those jeans." What she said threw me off my train of thought. I looked down. I had on my usual work clothes. An Atomic Sewer T-shirt, a pair of jeans and some black waterproof Timberland boots.

"Marcia, please. I sent you the flowers apologizing for my behavior, but you should have been the one apologizing. Now, I don't feel there is any way we can do any business together. There is no need for us to communicate."

"Darius. What is it, about eight inches?" She lowered her eyes to my crotch

I continued to speak until what she said finally registered. "What the fuck! Listen, Marcia, you're looking for a boy toy in the wrong place. I was getting frustrated. "Please get the fuck out!"

"Darius, please, calm down. I was just joking."

I had her in my world but she was taking over.

"Darius, how about we go away for a few days and you can think about what I can do for you? The connections I could plug you into."

84

"Don't you understand what "NO" means, Ms. Drake? I'm not interested in you. I don't give a fuck about your connections. I'm doing very well right now and don't need your bullshit. Please leave now." I walked over and opened the door for her. She stood and adjusted her skirt and jacket. Her face showed no emotion. She walked over to the door and grabbed my crotch, stretched up, and kissed me on the lips for a few seconds. She tried to slip me her tongue. I pushed her away.

Marcia adjusted her skirt and jacket again and said in a low voice," Mr. Miller, I usually get what I want and I want you. So one way or another, I'll get you to come around. So I'll just act like today never happened." She put two fingers in her mouth, sucked them, and slowly pulled them out until she got to the tips. She licked the tips of her fingernails and said, "Mmmm, Darius, you don't know what your missing. It feels bigger than I thought and I'm going to have fun with that taste you later." She then turned to walk away and put a little oomph into her walk. I felt like I just got punked and stood there for a few minutes before I slammed the door, walked to my desk and flipped it over.

Chapter 11

"Mr. Miller, are you okay?"

"What the fuck do you want? Get the fuck out." I was sitting in my chair with the desk still turned over. Valerie walked in and started picking up the mess. I was in a rage. I wanted to kill Ms. Marcia Drake. It felt like I was bitch slapped and she took my manhood.

"I'm sorry, Valerie. I'll clean this up."

"No. Mr. Miller. I think you should go home and relax."

"I think you're right, Valerie. I'm sorry I snapped at you."

"It's okay. I knew you were dealing with Ms. Drake. I just hope she's not under the desk." I pictured it in my mind and felt better. "Mr. Miller, don't worry. I'll take care of everything. Just go home.

"Thank you, Val." I kissed her on the cheek. "I'll call you later." I was almost out the door.

"Mr. Miller, Ms. Simmons had called and left a message for you to call her. Just the thought of Leslie was enough to lift my spirits. I got around to Old Patsy. I had left my cell phone on the front passenger seat. Leslie had called twice. I pushed redial.

"Hey Darius, sweetheart. I've been trying to call you all morning." I looked at my watch. I had been sitting in my office, pissed off, for over two hours. "I was about to call you and tell you that Paulie called and that he'll stop by the shop about twelve. So if you're not busy, could you please stop by and explain everything to him?"

The way she said "please" reminded me of my niece Shana. It brought a smile to my face. Maybe my day was starting to turn around.

"And Darius, I want you to promise me something."

"What, babe?"

"Keep your hands to yourself. I don't know if I can handle that again.

I smiled. She just gave me back my manhood.

"I'll try."

"Darius," Leslie said and hesitated a minute. "I think....well, I don't know Darius. I know we only met just recently and we've only known each other for a few days but I'm not sure if I should say it because I don't know how you feel, but

I love you." I felt lost. I fell silent for a few seconds. She let me off the hook again.

"You don't have to respond. That's just the way I feel. If you're not ready to say it, I understand."

"No. Leslie."

She interrupted me. "Darius don't say anything. I love you and that's enough for me. So I'll see you in an hour." I started to say goodbye but she giggled and hung up.

Chapter 12

I had enough time to run to Green Acres Mall and pick up some books. I wanted Leslie to read just a little something to help her understand the problem our culture is facing. A book by Tony Brown, one by Cornel West, also a book called 'How to Make the Political Process Work for the Black Race' by Rodney Daniels and one on business. Lastly, a handbook with three hundred words that were guaranteed to improve your vocabulary. I ran out the store and had to go back.

I was so interested in reeducating her that I almost forgot the study book for cosmetology exam. I added that to another book I had brought from home, How to Improve Your Self-Confidence. I was on my way to building my perfect woman. I thought my day was turning around until I turned the corner of her shop and Juice was leaning against his car, talking to some old brother. I got pissed again and almost kept going until I noticed Leslie standing in the doorway waving at me. I parked a few spaces in front of Juice. I took a deep breath and regained my composure. I was going to find out what was really up with this Juice character. I started walking up the block.

I looked at Juice and he said, "What's up." He extended his hand to shake mine, and his left hand at that to show me the fake Rolex. That made me feel better. The fool though it was real.

"What up, Darren."

I shook his hand. "No. its Darius."

      "Yeah that's right."

He must own at least a hundred tank tops because he was wearing another one. Green this time, with black jean shorts and brown and green Timberland boots. The brother he was with looked at me and said. "What's up, Darius? My name is Chillsnills."

"Excuse me?" I asked.

"Chillsnills." I looked confused. He said it again slowly. "Chills-nills."

I said, "Chillsnills."

He nodded his head; I must have got it right. "Yeah, man, the girls call me Chillsnills because I'm the shiznit."

Okay, that was more information than I needed to know. Chillsnills had to be kicking fifty in the ass. He had graying hair was cut low and slicked down. He was slim, some might say skinny. I couldn't say how his face looked because the hair hanging from his chin caught my attention. He had no mustache. No goatee. Just a small patch of hair about an inch long hanging for his chin, and not even in the middle. It was off to the left side of his chin and was streaked with gray.

"Nice to meet you, Chillsnills." I tried not to laugh in his face. I looked up and saw Leslie with her hand on her hips, watching me. She looked so good. I smiled and let go of Chillsnills hand and proceeded to the shop. Leslie was still in the doorway. She wore jeans that accented every curve of her hips and legs, a T-shirt with Total Experience Beauty Salon on it that fit her rather snugly, and her hair was in a ponytail. On the left side of her face. Just a few loose hairs dropped down to frame the left eye and its green outline glistered in the sun.

I hugged and kissed her. "Hey, baby, I missed you."

"I missed you too, Darius." She grabbed my hand and led me into the shop.

Where is everyone at?" I asked.

"Oh, I'm closed on Mondays, unless someone makes a request in advance with one of my girls." She led me to the beautician's chair. "Have a seat, baby. Let me trim you up."

I sat down and said, "I'm fine Leslie."

She rubbed by head. "I feel some hair. Let me shave it for you."

I didn't know what to say. I had a Samson complex. I didn't want any woman cutting my hair.

"No. I'm okay."

Before I could get the words out, she had the chair tilted back and was putting an apron around my neck. She must have seen the tension in my eyes." Relax, Darius. Trust me."

"I trust you, Leslie."

I tried my best to relax.

She whispered in my ear, "Breathe slowly and let the music take over your soul." I didn't even realize the music she had on was Musiq Soul child's 'Juslisen'. I leaned back and calmed my nerves. Okay, I must trust someone. That was, until she started sharpening the straight razor.

"Leslie, where are the clippers?" I asked, trying to sound calm.

"Trust me, Darius. I trusted you. She was a fast learner, using my line back at me. The thought of her not being able to pass her state board exam kept running through my mind and secondly, I hate the sight of blood, especially my own.

She kissed the top of my head, then rubbed shaving cream on it. It was warm and scented and felt good. She massaged it in. I calmed down after I noticed she had started on the left side of my head and my ear was still intact. She finished, then spun the chair around and adjusted it again, pushing the top side back at a greater angle. Leslie kissed me again, first on the forehead, then my cheek, and finally full on the lips. I reached up and grabbed her butt. She jumped back.

"No, Darius! Not now. Let me finish, plus Paulie should be here soon. So don't start something you can't finish." She said coyly.

I tried to respond but before I could get a word out, her lips were covering mine. I returned the favor with equal passion.

"Okay, Darius. That's enough." Leslie applied shaving cream to my face. She trimmed up my goatee, and then applied a facial cleanser and hot towel to my face.

"Now just relax for a few minutes and you're done."

It actually felt good, being treated like this. She removed the towel, adjusted the chair so I was sitting straight up, and then spun it so I could see the large mirror in front of the workstation. She did a good job. A damn good job.

"You like?" she asked. I nodded. "I like."

"Darius I...I...don't." Before she could finish the sentence, Juice walked in the door. "Leslie, may I speak to you for a minute," he asked.

"Sure, Juice. I'll be right back, Darius."

I gave her a slight smile. "Okay."

I watched her walk off. I didn't like the look in Juice's eyes and the wink he gave me only proceeded to piss me off. They walked outside and all I could do to control my anger was to hold my breath and count to twenty. That didn't work too well, so I got up and walked to the sink to splash my face with some cold water. I needed to find out once and for all what was the deal with her and Juice. I punched the wall and almost put my fist through it. Today was just not my day. I walked back over to the chair, leaned it back, and looked at the ceiling. I closed my eyes and Brenda popped up in my head, then her mother, then Marcia.

"Darius," Leslie's voice startled me.

"What's up with him?" I said too loud and with too much anger in my voice.

I caught her by surprise and I think I scared her because her eyes were wide. She shook her head for a minute and dropped it.

"Darius, I just told you over an hour ago that I love you. What do you think that I'm some slut? Baby, you think I'm playing some kind of game on you? I don't just give my heart to anyone. I knew it was too good to be true. I knew it was too fast. Just because of what I let you do to me, you think I'm some easy trick. I'm not and I never will be."

"Leslie, I'm sorry."

"Yes, Darius, you are."

"Leslie, please, I have love for you also, more than I care to admit. I was just jealous of him."

"Why, Darius? You're more of a man than he will ever be."

She went in her back pocket and pulled out an envelope and handed it to me.

"Darius I asked him to get me these." I took it and stared at it for a minute.

"Open it", she commanded. I turned it over in my hands a few times.

"Darius," she said. Her voice had pain in it. She looked like she wanted to cry.

"I wanted to surprise you." I opened the envelope and saw five tickets to Madison Square Garden for Saturday night. The WWE wrestling match between The Rock and Stone Cold Steve Austin. I felt low, real low.

"Leslie, you didn't have to."

"I know, but I wanted to." I looked at the five tickets and walked over to try and hug her.

She held me at arm's length and placed her hands in the middle of my chest.

"No. Darius. There is something I feel you should know. I did go out with Juice once, to a movie and dinner."

"I knew it! He wasn't hanging around for nothing."

"Don't say anything. Let me tell you everything. Juice owns the bodega across the street that's why he's always around here. He's been asking me out ever since I opened the shop. The more I turn him down, the harder he tries. He was always buying me gifts and stuff. I tried to return them but he wouldn't accept them. So I would give all the stuff to April. One Saturday night, I was closing up and he came over and helped me with the gates and asked if I wanted to go see a movie with him. I declined as usual, plus April was waiting for me in the car. He offered to take us both, so I asked April. I knew she was sort of interested in him so I thought it was a way to get the two of them together and keep him away from me. We went to see a movie and afterwards, to Red Lobster. After a few drinks Juice started talking about what he could do for me and what he wanted to do to me. Not only did it upset me, but he disrespected me and I got up to leave. He begged me to stay. April pulled me aside and we talked and she was able to talk me into staying. We finished the meal and all he did was talk about himself, all the women he was with and things he did for them and to them. He totally turned me off.

After dinner Juice wanted to go to a club. I declined and April accepted. They dropped me off home and went out to the club. They started seeing each other but he was still trying to hit on me. After about two months something happened between them and for some reason, April hates him. She would never tell me what happened. I notice the tension between April and Juice every time they're around each other. He still asks me out from time to time, but I refuse. He's just a friend and that's all he will ever be. So there is no reason to be jealous of him or anyone else."

I didn't know what to say. I just stood there, looking at the tickets.

"He has a friend who gets things, so when I came in this morning I asked him if he could get me the tickets. He sent Champagne to get them." I looked at her and still didn't know what to say.

"I was hoping Champagne didn't mention it to you when both of you were talking."

"I didn't talk to anyone named Champagne." I said.

Lisa looked at me strongly." Yes you did, before you came in."

I was lost for a second. Damn! "Chillsnills?" I asked.

"Yeah, Chillsnills. I guess that's what he's calling himself now." Chillsnills, Champagne; an old-assed man still using nicknames.

"I'm sorry, Leslie. Will you forgive me?" She came over and hugged me, then gave me a long stare and kissed me.

"Can we please keep this rated PG," a voice from behind me called out.

"Paulie. What's up?"

"I came to see the changes you came up with." He walked and shook hands with Leslie first, then me. I tapped his stomach, which was stretching his R.A.F shirt.

"Time for a diet, Paulie."

"Not me," was his response. "I can eat like a horse and I'm as strong as an ox. How many fifty year olds you know still making babies?" He had me; not many.

I took Paulie next door and gave him the layout of everything I wanted done. Leslie just

Followed behind us, watching. I had it all figured out. Total Experience Day Salon was going to be an adventure.

"I can start tomorrow and have everything done in thirty days."

Leslie looked at me and grabbed my hand in excitement. "How much is this going to cost." she asked.

"Don't worry, Ms. Simmons. Not much more. Not with Big D here doing all the plumbing."

She squeezed my hand. "Alright, Paulie. Can you start tomorrow?"

"Fine with me. I'll be here at 7:30 a.m. Will you be here to let me in Ms. S.?"

"Sure. No problem."

"Okay, everything's settled, then. Oh, D, your neighbor, Mr. Johnson asked me to remind you that he expects to see you Saturday night." Paulie reminded me

I forgot about his dinner party Saturday. Damn, there goes Stone Cold and The Rock.

"Sure, Paulie, I remember."

"Okay, see you tomorrow at 7:30 in the morning, Ms. Simmons."

"I'm sorry, Leslie. I forgot about the appointment."

"Its okay, Darius. Maybe next time."

Chapter 13

"Don't worry, Mom. Tracy will be alright."

"Darius, she has four kids out there at the Garden. It's a mad house."

"Mom, she can handle them. It's not like it's the first time she took them all out together. Old lady, I asked if you wanted me to get you a ticket so you could join them."

The phone line got quiet. "Boy, you know I'm not into that wrestling stuff."

"Mom, trust me. She'll be alright."

"Darius, who is this Leslie woman you've been spending so much time with? I haven't seen you all week."

"What's the matter, you getting jealous?"

"No, stupid, but its not often you miss a whole week without raiding my refrigerator." She was definitely being a mother.

"Mom, I'll bring her by soon to meet you."

"Hmm. DJ can't stop talking about her and his truck."

"Mom, I'll bring her around soon to meet you, okay?"

"Oh, I get to meet this one and she's spending time with your son. This must be serious."

"No, Mom, we just met, really. Once you meet her, you'll like her."

"Oh, I see. Okay, I want to meet her soon. One last thing Darius, what about Tracy?"

"What do you mean?"

"Tracy is in love with you."

"Mom, stop it. She's like a little sister."

"Darius, it's your life. All I want is for you to be happy with whomever you're pleased to be with. Now, call me tomorrow."

" Bye, Mom."

Tracy's in love with me? I held the phone for a minute before I hung up. No, I would have noticed by now. When I gave her the tickets for the wrestling match, all she did was hug me. No, Mom was reaching.

I looked in my bedroom mirror. I let Leslie trim me up this morning and I looked damn good. I had on black linen pants, a black linen shirt and black sandals. Damn, I looked good if I did say so my myself. I had to stop admiring myself because the phone started to ring.

"Hello?"

"Hey, Darius," Tracy answered,

"Tracy is everything okay? Are the kids alright?"

"Stop, Darius. I just called to let you know everything is all right and to enjoy yourself and don't rush back home tomorrow. I can handle the kids."

"Are you sure, Tracy?"

"Yes, Darius. Plus, I have Old Patsy. I'll probably go to the movies or to the park. Don't worry. I'll see you tomorrow night."

"If you insist. Thanks Tracey, I owe you big time. I'll leave some money on the dresser and be careful. Oh, and Tracy, don't keep Shana and Michael all day.

"Drop them off at my mom's house."

"Darius, I'll be okay."

"Tracy?"

"Bye, Darius." She hung the phone up before I could finish talking.

I went back to the mirror to admire myself but I couldn't shake the thought of Tracy being in love with me. I didn't see it. She was like a sister. Her actions never suggested anything to me and I know I would have picked it up by now. Mom was seeing things. I was brought back to reality by the phone ringing again.

"Hello?" I heard Leslie's voice and all thoughts of Tracy vanished.

"Darius, do you realize this is the first night I will not see you in a week? Why don't you stop by the shop before you leave? I miss you."

"Miss me?" My head started to swell up and a big smile crossed my face.

"How could you miss me and I saw you this morning?" The smile got deeper and I did a little dance step. Everything was working as planned. "Okay, I'll stop by if you can answer three questions."

"Oh come on Darius, you've been drilling me all week. School is closed on the weekends," she answered in a pouty voice.

"You know the shop is really out of my way, "I lied.

"Alright, Darius, three questions."

"Alright. The first one is, what is an esthetician and what do they do?" The phone line was silent for a moment. "Leslie?"

"Yes, Darius, give me a second. Okay, Darius. An esthetician, which is also spelled with an "A", specializes in the care of the skin, particularly the face. By the way, you pronounced it wrong."

"Okay, question number two. What is micro plantation?"

"Well, Mr. Miller, if you're going to test me, get it right. Its micro implantation derma pigmentation or, in simplest terms, permanent make-up, which is almost the same as a tattoo. It can be applied by hand or with two machines: the coil machine and the rotary machine. The coil machine is best for eyebrows and outlining lips. The rotary machine is good for adding color to the skin. For instance, if a person has light spots or if they want a mole added."

I was impressed! I had been drilling Leslie all week and she was retaining everything. I had no doubt in my mind that she was going to pass the state board exam this time.

"Okay, Ms. Simmons, last question. How are black people being robbed with the new rule added to the census count?" I knew I had her because I just read it in the new issue of Black Enterprise. The phone was silent.

"Leslie, you have ten seconds." I started to hum the theme to Jeopardy. "Oh, I'm sorry Leslie, your time is up but we do have some nice consolation prizes for you. "The phone stayed quiet. "Leslie?"

"Yes, Darius?"

"I'll call you tomorrow."

"You're really not going to come and see me?"

"You couldn't answer the third questions. A deal is a deal."

She sounded depressed. "Okay, Darius. You want to make a deal? If I get the right answer, I want you to buy dinner for everyone in the shop tonight."

"And Leslie, what do I get if you lose?"

"Use your imagination. Anything you want, Darius."

A big smile spread across my face. The possibilities that popped in my head were all X- rated.

"Okay, Leslie, deal."

"Because of the number of undocumented people living in our communities, the government could never get an accurate count. Therefore, we are short-changed on money coming into the community and when new voting districts are drawn up, we lose adequate representation."

"Damn, good answer, but that's not the one I was looking for."

"Okay, Darius, whatever. Have a good time tonight. Call me tomorrow."

"Leslie?"

"Yes, Darius.

I was about to tell her I was going to come anyway but changed my mind. "I'll call you in the morning." I said and hung up.

She did quite well. I wouldn't have gotten the last one myself if I hadn't read Black Enterprise.

Chapter 14

I hadn't driven my Benz in months and it started up on the first try. Precision craftsmanship at its best. The inch of dust was a surprise because I always kept it covered. It was nothing two minutes at the brushless car wash couldn't cure. I usually liked to hand wash it but not the way I was dressed now. I'm not a real car buff. I don't even remember the color. Don't get me wrong, I know what color it is but the official name of it, I could never remember. It's a light mint green mixed with silver with a black convertible top. It was custom painted for someone and that person never came back to pick it up. Me personally knowing the owner of the dealership, I got it at a very good price. I loved the color and bought it because it was different. It was a nice night to ride with the top down or as Nas said, "With the titties out."

The car wash was only about seven blocks from Leslie's salon, so I had an excuse to drop in on her. I was going to do it anyway but I didn't want her to think that she could always get her way. I wanted her to be independent but not snobby with it. If I gave in to her every time she called then she would be in control and no one dictated my moves. For a change, the carwash line wasn't around the corner but there was still a wait. My mind drifted again. Everything was going well since Monday. No Marcia, no Brenda, which was real good. Every night with Leslie this week had been too good to be true. She was so eager to learn that she digested almost every book that I brought her and had some questions that almost stumped me. If it weren't for the attendant tapping on the window, I wouldn't have noticed that I had already been through the wash.

"I'm sorry boss," I said, somewhat embarrassed. I pulled around to the front lot, dropped the top and got out to get a good look at a job well done. The evening sun caught the rims and almost blinded me. This car was just beautiful. I didn't know much about it though. Damn, all I knew how to do was fix a flat. I didn't know the engine size or any of the questions most men asked. I just knew that my car turned heads. At the same time I was admiring my car, three young ladies were passing by. I didn't know if they were checking my Benz or me out. It didn't matter 'cause they were too young. That didn't stop me from giving them a wink.

As I started the engine, the young ladies stopped. I pulled up in front of them and the one in the middle waved at me. She looked like she was about sixteen, so I said hello and pulled off. I noticed the disappointment on her face but I wasn't going out like that.

The car wash was on the corner of Springfield and Linden Blvd, right across from a Mickey D's. There was a small group of teenagers pointing at the car while I waited for the traffic light to turn green. Once I turned the corner, my good feeling changed with the sight of flashing lights behind me. The "boys" were rolling and a black man in an expensive car must be a drug dealer. I'm not stupid, though. The way they were assaulting and killing black people and getting away with it made me hit the # key and number 3 on my cell phone and plug in the speaker.

"Put your hands where I can see them," the young white cop said with his hand on his gun. He looked to be about twenty, 6'2"or 6'3", very thin and could tip the scale at maybe 140 lbs. soaking wet with a pocket full of rocks. He must have watched too many episodes of COPS on TV growing up. He had his legs spread wide with a stupid look on his face, like he was trying to be mean, but I could see the fear in his blue eyes. His partner was on the passenger side, looking over the car. He was the opposite: 5'9", maybe 5'10", thick around the torso, thinning gray hair and a bulbous nose. He had the look of a heavy drinker, his brown eyes were blood shot.

The rookie spoke up again, "Whose car is this?"

That question pissed me off. "Officer I'm going to reach slowly into my back pocket and take out my wallet. I repeat, I'm taking out my wallet so please don't get nervous. I don't want anyone to get hurt." I pulled out my wallet and handed him my driver's license.

"Now officer, I'm going to reach into my glove compartment and get the registration slowly. Remember, I don't want anyone to get hurt." I reached in and grabbed the registration and insurance card. His partner didn't say a word and just watched.

"Darius," the rookie said.

"No, it's Mr. Miller." I caught him off guard.

"Okay, Mr. Miller. You're from Mountainville, New York?"

"Yes." He wasn't going to get any explanation from me.

"What are you doing down here?"

"Excuse me, officer. This is a free country and I can drive anywhere I want. Now, if I did anything wrong, then give me a ticket and I will see you in court."

"No, Darius, it's just a routine traffic stop," he explained.

"Well, Officer, racial profiling is against the law so the excuse of routine traffic stop is no longer valid. If you don't mind giving me your name and badge number so I could report this to your captain. And it's Mr. Miller."

The rookie looked confused and tried to speak but couldn't. He looked over at his partner for help but got no response.

"Darius, do you mind if we search your car?" the rookie said, finally finding his voice.

"No, you can't. What is your probable cause?" Before I could finish my thought, the answer from the speaker finished it for me.

"My client will not get out of the car and you are violating his civil rights. Everything you have said has been recorded so if you want to continue to harass Mr. Miller, I will have you brought up on charges and you will be ticketing sleighs up in Alaska. So dress warm."

The rookie was visibly shaking but his partner asked calmly, "Whom may I ask is talking?"

"This is Morris Goldstein, attorney at law and a close personal friend of the Queen's D.A. Now, Officer, may I have your name and shield number for my records. Please cooperate because if I have to look up any reports for traffic stops and waste my time any further, then the penalties will be very extensive. So just cooperate, gentlemen."

The rookie blurted out his name and shield number and his partner reluctantly did the same.

"We're sorry to bother you, Mr. Miller," the rookie said as he handed me back my license and paperwork and stood there in a moment of indecisiveness.

When I started the car, I had to ask him to move so I could pull out. "Morris, thank God you were home."

"Darius, what was all that about?"

"D.W.B. that's all."

"What?" Morris asked."

"Driving While Black."

"Okay, I understand. Those papers you talked about with me are finished. I'm not too sure you should follow through with them but you can pick them up Monday morning.

Also, are you coming to the Johnson's dinner party?"

"Yeah, Morris, I'll make it. Actually, I'm just going to make one quick stop and then I'm on my way over there.

"Okay Darius, I'll see you soon."

Morris Goldstein was a great lawyer and a good friend. He had drawn up papers for Brenda to sign so there wouldn't be any more claims of her needing money. Basically, she would get four grand a month for DJ and I would pay for his education and clothes. She couldn't contest it any more and if she did, my company was registered as a limited liability corporation, or LLC. DJ was the CEO and I was the President. When the courts looked up and saw that DJ owned everything already and I just ran the business and looked out for his well being, then me being the parent who claimed him on my income taxes and handled all the banking transactions was the one who was in control. So Brenda loses all the way around. She couldn't complain, considering that four grand a month for food was a great deal.

Chapter 15

Pulling up in front of Leslie's shop made my mood positive again. There was very little sunlight out, just enough to catch the expression on Juice's face when he noticed it was me. His expression changed from surprised to anger to envy so fast that I had to laugh.

I stepped out of the car and stood there a second so that Juice could get a good look, then proceeded to walk around the car. I was met on the other side by a vision of beauty.

She extended her hand, which I took.

"Hello, my name is Natalie. Nice to meet you."

"Hello, my name is Darius." I released her hand and took a step back. I was too close to really enjoy her womanly curves.

She was 5'6", very well proportioned, thick legs, with very smooth honey brown skin. Her legs looked great and I was getting a damn good look because the gray skirt wasn't covering much as my eyes moved up ever so slowly. She had on what looked like one of DJ's shirts. Her exposed mid-section displayed a tattoo that framed her belly button, which contained a diamond navel ring. I couldn't tell where the tattoo started because her skirt covered that section but it did continue up towards her cantaloupe-sized breasts. The shirt collar was cut so it sported a V dip in the front almost to her nipples. I wasn't sure that's where the tattoo ended. Hell, for all I knew that could have been the beginning. Slowly working my way up and I mean very slowly, I saw that she had thick seductive lips and a nose that was slightly upturned at the tip like a Caucasian's.' She had almond-shaped hazel eyes and her face was framed by long, silky black hair with red highlights. At the moment I started to feel guilty because I had just sinned. In my heart, Natalie was a beauty to behold but she lacked something Leslie has, and that's style and class. I wondered if she would have even looked my way had I been driving Old Patsy or my work truck. I hoped so but I would never know.

"Darius, what are you doing tonight? I'm not busy." Natalie's smile was very generous as she turned sideways so I could get a look at her well-shaped ass. I said damn to myself and then got my mind back on track.

"I have plans," I answered. She looked at me like she was used to getting what she wanted and couldn't believe I turned her down. "Natalie, I'm seeing someone and as beautiful as you are, and the temptation is there, I could never disrespect her in that way."

"Okay, Darius. But what she doesn't know won't hurt her." Natalie said with a very seductive smile and licked her lips.

"You are so right, but I'll know and that's the problem."

"That's so sweet," was her response," but if you change your mind, call me." She pulled out a business card from heaven knows where, handed it to me, smiled and walked off. I thought, what you don't' know won't hurt you. I learned the hard way that what you don't' know may kill you. I dropped her card because I had no use for it. I noticed Juice was watching so I hit my car alarm and walked toward the shop.

"Hello, April, how are you? April looked up and smiled. That gold tooth was so much of a turn off. I wanted to snatch it out.

"I'm feeling great, Mr. Miller. I love the improvement you came up with for next door. It's going to be great! I'm so excited."

"So am I, April, Is Leslie in?"

"Yes. She's in her office. For the past week all she does is stay back there and read. You know the way, Mr. Miller."

"Thank you, April." The shop was empty compared to the way I'd seen it before. I said hello to the few people that were there. I knocked on the door, waiting for Leslie's response and staying quiet at the same time. I waited a few seconds and knocked again.

"Who's there?"

I proceeded to knock again but the door opened.

"I have to talk to DJ. It seems he's been giving away a lot of his T-shirts."

Leslie had surprised look on her face. Before she could respond, I put my lips on hers. She returned the favor but then suddenly stopped and pushed me away.

"What are you doing here?" she said.

"You lost the bet and told me to use my imagination. Anything I want, and I want you with me tonight. You're going to a dinner."

"My hair's a mess, Darius and I'm not dressed."

"You look damn good to me." Her T-shirt wasn't as tight as Natalie's but it fit snug and was just short enough to show her belly button. Plus, with those form-fitting jeans, I had to fight myself to keep my hands off her. I just grabbed her hand. "Let's go."

"But Darius, I can't. The shop…"

I paid her no attention and kept pulling.

She didn't resist much. I got to April's desk. "April, would you mind closing up the shop tonight?"

"No problem, Mr. Miller."

"Please call me Darius."

No. Darius, "Leslie whined," I have to drive April home."

I went in my wallet and handed April a hundred-dollar bill. "Here's cab fare and dinner money." I proceeded to pull Leslie outside. Once outside I spun her around and said, "Trust me."

"Darius," I didn't respond. I just led her toward the car. She looked at the car in astonishment. "You're driving this?"

"Yes," was all I said? I opened the door and helped her in. I had black floor mats with my initials, D.M., engraved in gray. They matched my gray leather interior perfectly.

"But Darius, I'm not dressed for this."

"Trust me, Leslie you'd make a potato sack look good."

It was getting late when I pulled in front of Macy's at Green Acres Mall. I gave her my American Express Card. "Leslie, it's not formal. It's actually a catered barbecue. Buy some shoes and a nice dress. I'll meet you in the women's department in about fifteen minutes."

Leslie looked at me, then at the card. "Darius, I have clothes at home. Take me home and I can get dressed there." I reminded her that it was whatever I wanted. For a woman she shopped quickly, which was another plus for her. We were out of the mall and on the Cross Island Parkway headed toward the Whitestone Bridge within a half an hour.

What does an electrologist do?"

"No, Darius. It's Saturday. Please, no more questions."

It was very warm Saturday night. We had the top down and Leslie's eyes seemed to out glow the stars in the sky.

"Listen Leslie, the test is only two weeks away, so the day of the week doesn't matter. It's what you know when that test ends that matters. When you want something, you have to do anything and everything to get it. If that means studying on Satur-

115

day night and going to church and praying to God on Sunday, then so be it."

She didn't respond for a few seconds and then said softly, "An electrologist specializes in the removing of unwanted hair."

I was pushing a little too hard. "Okay, Leslie, no more questions tonight." That brought a smile to her face. "Darius, where are we going? I thought we were going to your neighbor's house."

"We are."

"But Darius, you don't live over here."

Over where? I said in a joking way. We had just passed over the Whitestone Bridge and through the Cross-Bronx up the Bronx River Parkway.

Where ever we are."

"Yes, I do." She looked at me with a very inquisitive expression. "You've been to my apartment, but now we are going to my house."

She still looked confused. "Lay back and relax, Leslie. I'll explain once we get there."

She started to say something but I touched her thigh and repeated, "Relax and enjoy the ride. We have about an hour to go."

Chapter 16

Leslie looked so peaceful curled up in the front seat of my car. I could have watched her sleep all night. I know only God can create a woman, so I hope He doesn't mind me making a few adjustments. Maybe just a little customizing.

"Leslie, baby, wake up. Leslie, wake up." I had to nudge her a few times before she showed any signs of life. It had been a long week for both of us. We were at the shop late every night. I did the plumbing and she was my helper. At the same time I drilled her on just about everything on her state exam. I knew it enough to ace it myself. Leslie slowly came to life.

"Where are we?" She asked, rubbing the sleep out of her eyes.

"This is my home."

She looked around. "What do you mean, your house? It looks like we're in some type of park."

"Well, actually, we are. My land is 9.5 acres. The state owns everything after that. They have acres of trails, scenic views and waterfalls from my back porch. You can see the Catskill Mountains, the Shawangunk Ridge and parts of Connecticut."

"Darius, where are we?"

Mountainville, New York." The puzzled look on her face told me she didn't know what I was talking about. "This is Mountainville, NY in Orange County, about an hour and forty-five minutes from the city. It's mostly a collection of executive homes and quaint restored Victorian farmhouses. This town is so small that they don't even have mail delivery. I have to drive over to the general store, which has a post office in the rear, in order to get my mail."

I rolled the car up about five feet and the motion lights activated, illuminating the house.

Leslie's jaw dropped in amazement.

"Do you like it?"

"Darius, this is yours?"

"Yep."

"How can you afford this?"

"I'll explain it to you later."

"Darius please don't tell me you sell drugs."

"No, Leslie, I would never sell drugs." I got a little up-set at her comment. A black man with a nice car and home was always considered a drug dealer, basketball player or rapper.

She noticed the agitation in my voice. "I'm sorry, Darius but this house is incredible! How can you afford it?"

I guess it was time to tell Leslie everything. "Leslie, I own the company and I own about ten buildings. I rent them out to the city for tenants who are HIV-positive or infected with full-blown AIDS. They give me about two thousand a month for each apartment. Each building has at least four apartments, so you do the math."   She started adding on her fingers and suddenly stopped. "Darius, I need a calculator for that. So when was you going to tell me about all this?"

"I'm telling you now. I own this, but I don't really own any of it."

A confused look crossed her face. "How could you own it and not really own it?

"Everything I own belongs to my sons. The buildings and the one with my apartment in it are all in my son Darien's name. I'm just protecting his interests. DJ owns atomic Sewer and Drain Cleaning. Basically, I work for them and they provide me with a home and a job." I noticed that I had lost her. "I'll explain it to you later. It's almost eleven. I want to drop in on the Johnson's party, make my presence known and get out as quick as possible."

My front door has a keyless entry system. I pressed the combination and the door opened.

"Darius, what did you just do?" Leslie asked. "Where is the door knob?"

"I don't need one." I showed her the brass plate and the keypad with the brass numbers.

"All I have to do is press the code and the door springs open."

"Oh, I forgot something in the trunk. Go right in, Leslie, it'll only take me a few seconds." I went to the trunk and re-trieved the items I needed. When I got back, Leslie was still standing by the front door.

"Why didn't you go in?" I asked.

"The lights," she replied.

I walked in and the foyer lit up. "I have motion sensors in the foyer and living room. So there is no need to feel for a light switch."

The first thing that caught Leslie's eyes was the solid marble staircase leading to the second floor. I could see she was totally impressed. I had to nudge her. "Leslie, I need you to get dressed. I don't want to get stuck over at the Johnson's too long."

"Oh, okay, Darius. Where is your shower? I need about fifteen minutes to get ready." I gave her a look like she was cra-zy. I didn't have to say a word.

"Okay, about a half an hour," she amended. I didn't know a woman alive who could shower and dress in fifteen minutes. I led her up the steps and the oak floors throughout the top floor shined in the semi-darkness. I hit the hallway light and increased the glow. I tugged her hand gently.

"I'll give you the grand tour when we get back, I promise." Leslie was trying to take it all in and I didn't have time for that right now. "The shower's to the left." I pointed as we entered the master bedroom. "Everything you need is in the bathroom." I dropped the bags on the bed.

"One second. Let me show you how to use the shower."

"Darius, I know how to work a shower." I smiled to myself and counted to ten, as I heard her fumble with the pipes in the bathroom "Darius, how do I turn on the water on?" I walked in and she was blushing.

"This is a full body shower with a nozzle covering all angles and one nozzle straight overhead."

The controls were right next to the built-in soap dish. They were like radio dials. Each of the nozzles has its own switch. The water started out warm and you increased or decreased the temperature by sliding a lever left or right. I explained everything to Leslie but she still looked confused, so I set everything up for her except the overhead nozzle. Black women's hair kinked up when it got wet and resulted in their hairdo getting fucked up. I once dated a young lady and after three hours of great sex she told me I owed her $150 because I sweated out her hairdo. She explained the whole water thing to me. I gave her the money and never saw her again.

"Darius, I thought you were in a rush! Get out and let me shower, and no peeking!" Leslie said with a mischievous smile. I closed the door and opened all the bags and laid out the clothes she purchased. $650 for a dress, some shoes and a matching bag. Oh, I couldn't forget the bra and panties too. I also laid out my surprise. The shower had stopped and I didn't even hear Leslie enter the room.

"Darius, do you mind if I get dressed?"

I came back out of my trance, my imagination tended to wander from time to time.

"Ahh yes...excuse me. I'll be downstairs. Just yell if you need anything."

"Darius, what is this?" She noticed my little surprise. "It's....

"Before I could respond she stated, "I know what it is but where did it come from is what I'm asking?"

I couldn't read the expression on her face.

"I bought it."

"Okay, Darius, for whom?"

Now the expression on my face was very readable. "I bought it for you when you went into Macy's. I went inside Victoria's Secret and purchased it and put it in trunk before I met you inside. You didn't think I was giving you lingerie that some other woman wore?"

"I don't know." Leslie put it up against her body and checked it out. I was hoping the towel she had wrapped around her would fall, but my luck wasn't that good. I went back to imagining how Leslie's body could put the stitching to a test. I bought it a little tight on purpose. The crotch less panties and teddy with the low-cut breast cups had my mind spinning.

"But Darius, who said we were going to do anything?"

My mind just suddenly stopped. I lost all train of thought. It was like a car going a hundred miles an hour and then instantly hitting the brakes. I felt my manhood slowly growing soft. She smiled and my heart began to beat again. I had to get out of the room quick or we would never see John and Mary Johnson. I walked over and took the lingerie from her balled it up and threw it in the corner before I looked at my watch. "Please, babe, can you get dressed? I'll meet you downstairs," and kissed her cheek. My erection returned to full force.

Leslie still had a puzzled look on her face. "Darius, why did you do that?" She looked at me, then at the lingerie. "I'm just testing it." She still looked puzzled.

I'll explain my theory once I see you in it. Its not going to take me long to get you out of it, ball it up and throw it in the corner. So that was just practice. Plus, I won the bet. You said to use my imagination. Anything I want. And I want you!"

"Double or nothing." Leslie taunted.

I smiled. "What else do you want to lose?"

"Okay, Darius, if I lose, and then I'll wear that thing you bought and also be your love slave for the rest of the weekend."

Not only was I erect but also my heart was fluttering. I had to breathe slow and hesitate before I answered her. I didn't want to seem too excited. I'd been with plenty of women, more than I cared to count. Not that I could keep an accurate count, but there had been a lot. For some reason, Leslie had me hooked.

"Okay Leslie, bet."

She paused and said, "Here is the answer for that last question you asked; for every black man incarcerated, does it collectively lower our economic value for jobs lost and socially cripples our home and devastate our family structure?"

"No," I answered, trying to hold in my happiness.

She threw a pillow at me and said, "Darius get out so I can get dressed."

I smiled as I walked out, and wanted to dance. Shit, I almost wanted to sing.

Chapter 17

The spotlight gave the Johnson's home a movie premiere look. I had never seen the device up close. It really didn't serve any purpose unless you were trying to flag down passing spaceships. The driveway, or what used to be the driveway, was now a hardwood floor with a plush red carpet down the middle. Before we could get out of the car, a young man was at Leslie's door. He supplied valet parking. I was impressed. He had opened Leslie's door and then closed it gently. He ran around the back and carefully opened my door. When I got out I looked at him straight in his face. I tried not to stare but it was impossible. His face was very thin and very pale. His nose was straight, long, and narrow with extremely small lips. It looked like it would hurt him to talk. His eyes seemed to stick out just as far as his nose. They were blue and they pulled me in. I looked down and passed him my keys and a twenty-dollar bill. I felt bad for staring at him but he said thank you, jumped in the car and rode off with his stringy blond hair blowing in the wind.

I grabbed Leslie's hand and followed the red carpet path around to the side of the house. At the rear of the house, the carpet gave way to high gloss polished wood floor that was covered by a huge white tent, with a chandelier hanging high in the middle. Leslie squeezed my hand tightly. He palms were sweating. She was out of her element.

I brought her hand up and kissed it. "Relax, baby. We're not staying long."

"Darius, what am I going to say? I can't talk to these people. I have nothing in common with them. You've been teaching me about black culture; I don't know what to say to these white people."

"Just relax. You'll be fine." I reassured her.

The place was packed. I noticed the mayor of New York talking to Marcia. I tried to turn fast but when she called my name, I knew there was no way to avoid her this evening. Might as well get it over with. I grabbed Leslie's hand and walked through the crowd.

"Hello Ms. Drake."

Darius, have you ever had the pleasure of meeting the mayor of the world's greatest city?"

The mayor just smiled as I shook his hand and introduced him to Leslie. She extended her hand to shake his but he raised it up to his lips and kissed it. He commented on Leslie's dress and her beauty. I scanned the place for one of our hosts to rescue me from the inevitable.

"Dance with me, Darius," Marcia demanded.

Damn it! I looked to Leslie for some help but she was taken in by what the mayor was saying.

Marcia leaned over to Leslie. "Do you mind if I steal Darius away for a moment?

I don't mind." Leslie answered. Damn it! Damn it!

Marcia grabbed my hand and led me over to where the band was playing. There were more people standing around talking and drinking than dancing. We were outside in a covered tent with a five-foot section cut out and I was sweating bullets. The band was playing what sounded like something slow R. Kelly: "...I want to go half on a baby..." Where the hell did that come from? I put my arm around Marcia and kept a respectable distance from her but she had other plans. She grabbed my left butt cheek and pulled me closer.

"Marcia, have some respect for me, my date and for yourself."

"Why don't you get rid of her, spend the night with me?"

I grinned at her and said, "Fuck you, hell no."

The music changed and it seemed that they were playing something up tempo. Marcia released her grip on my butt and backed up. She wore a beige dress with buttons down the front. Only the top five buttons were buttoned and she opened

127

them and removed her dress. The first thing that caught my eyes was her nipples. Under the dress, she wore something just as sheer as the lingerie I had just bought Leslie. It was black and I could see everything. It clung to her body as she danced. She didn't want anyone to know that she wasn't a natural blond so she'd shaved her pubic region. She spun around so I could get a good look and started to dance in front of me very seductively.

I was harder than a roll of quarters but twice as long. I know everyone noticed because Marcia was attracting a crowd. My feet felt like lead. I couldn't move and my mind reacted slowly. She was up on me, slowly rubbing her ass against me and I just stood there, stunned. She brought me back to reality with a kiss on my lips. I thought, fuck being civil, and pushed her off. Marcia hit the ground ass first. She was alright; the only thing that was hurt was her feelings and her pride. I turned and everyone was staring. I saw Leslie standing next to Paulie and Mary Johnson. I grabbed her arm and dragged her out front.

"Darius, it's alright," she said, trying to console me.

"No, its not, Leslie. She disrespected you and me, and I'm not going to let anyone hurt you in any way."

"Darius, she was drunk," Mrs. Johnson explained.

I gave her a look but she smiled at me and melted my anger. I walked over to her and gave her a friendly kiss.'

"Leslie, the only one I want to dance for me is you."

Chapter 18

The ride back home was spent in silence. I knew what I did to Ms. Drake was going to come back and bite me in the ass.

"Are you alright Darius?" Leslie asked.

"What?" I replied.

"Are you alright"

"Why do you ask?"

"Because we have been sitting in the car for a few minutes and we're here."

I came out of my daze and shut the engine off. I'm sorry, Leslie."

"Don't worry about it. By tomorrow you'll forget about it." She put her hand on my upper right thigh and she was right, because my manhood responded and all thoughts went back to Leslie.

I gave her a kiss on the cheek. "Thank you, Ms. Simmons" I got out and ran around the car to open her door. "Really, Leslie, I'm sorry. I never told you how beautiful you look."

"Thank you, Darius and I must admit you look quite handsome yourself. Almost good enough to eat."

I smiled. "Almost? You don't' know what you're missing."

We walked to the front door of my house and as soon as I opened the door, Leslie pushed me against the wall, partially opened my shirt and kissed my chest. She reached up and kissed me with so much passion that I nearly exploded. She broke our embrace and rubbed my chest while kissing each nipple lightly and slowly from left to right. She then unbuckled my belt and threw it on the floor, which made my pants slide down to my ankles. I took my shirt off and dropped in on the floor and stepped out of my pants. She relieved me of my boxer shorts and I stood there naked as the day I was born. She stood back and looked at me, which made me a little uncomfortable. I pulled her closer but mini-me was standing at attention. I had to push him up against my stomach so she could get closer. I kissed her with so much passion that my erection was throbbing. I almost ripped her dress trying to get at her breasts.

"Wait, Darius, let me help you." Leslie pulled the little black dress up slowly over her hips and gave a little wiggle. It got stuck partly over her breasts so she gave another little wiggle. It looked so sexy that I bit my bottom lip and put my hands behind my back so I wouldn't grab her. She looked toward the loving room for a place to set her dress.

"Just drop it," I said."

"No, Darius, be patient. We have all night."

As Leslie walked away I admired every curve of her body and then thought about Brenda. Why was her ass so flat? She couldn't fill out a pair of panties. There always seemed to be extra material, like a baby with oversized Pampers. The thought of Brenda had mini-me going limp so I looked at Leslie for positive reinforcement and he happily responded. She had removed her bra and was in the process of removing her panties. She looked at me and winked and proceeded to do a sexy little wiggle from side to side as she removed them slowly, inch by inch.

My mind was racing and I couldn't take it. I covered the twenty-five feet or so that distanced us in about five steps. I took her hand and led her to the kitchen. "One minute," I told her and ran into the hallway, almost slipping on the hardwood floor. I didn't realize that I still had socks on. I ran up the cold stone stairs, taking them three at a time. I grabbed some sheets and towels out of the linen closet and returned back down, taking two giant leaps. I was back in the kitchen and Leslie was looking around.

"This place is nice."

I put my lips over hers and kissed her gently. "We can tour the place later," I said in between kisses.

I walked over to the kitchen table, which was marble with a clear glass cover to protect the surface. I put two or three towels over it and covered them with the sheet and walked back over to Leslie. She had a puzzled look on her face. I looked at her and before I could say a word she said, "Trust you. Right."

I nodded my head, picked her up and laid her on the table. I went to the fridge, got some honey, whipped cream and some ice. I returned to the table and she looked at the supplies.

"Again, trust you, right," she repeated. I just winked and adjusted her body so her legs were hanging off the table and her treasure chest was at the end of the table.

"This is uncomfortable Darius."

"One second." I took two towels, folded them and laid them on the floor so I could kneel down. "Now put your feet on my shoulders." I spread her legs and started to probe her with my fingers, working her into a slight frenzy.

"Darius," Leslie said in a breathless voice. "Darius!" Her body started to inch closer to the end of table. I removed my fingers and tasted her. I took my finger and exposed the full clitoris and licked it slowly. Right behind it, at the shallow end of the clitoris, is a very sensitive nerve. I read about it so I licked it slowly, then hard, then harder, then slowly, then I covered it with my mouth and sucked it slowly, then fast, then slowly again. I must have been doing it right because Leslie was calling on the Holy Spirit, I think. What she was saying I couldn't understand, like she was speaking in tongues. I turned it up a notch and reached back in and hit her. A spot, then the G spot while still tongue wrestling with her clitoris. I thought I did hear her say something that resembled my name. Leslie was arching her back and shaking convulsively. She wrapped her legs around my head.

"D-a-r-i-u-s!" I knew I had hit the right spot then. Leslie's hands were reaching down for my head and tried to push my head in her vagina.

"Darius, I..." Before she could get the rest of the sentence out I unlocked her left leg from around my head, I rose up and entered her. Her breathing paused and she looked up at me. I blew her a kiss and she closed her eyes as I stroked it slow. Back and forth from the tip to the base, slowly, one half an inch at a time. I took some ice and it almost immediately melted as I massaged her nipples with it. First the left then the right. I left a trail of water across her chest and when the ice cube got too small, I rubbed her smooth stomach with it and let the sliver of ice rest in her belly button. I increased the pace and worked her into frenzy. "Oh God, Darius, oh God, Darius," Leslie yelled.

I think I could have yelled it myself because I was so lost in the pleasure. Her legs were getting tight around my waist. "Darius, give it all to me. I love you, Darius and I don't ever want this to end. "Oh God, Darius, YES!" I unhooked her legs and raised those arms length apart and worked all angles. I didn't want to miss a spot. "I'm on the pill let it go... I am almost there!" She screamed. I increased the speed and brought myself to the point of no return. "Darius I'm coming, please Darius cum with me!"

It felt like I blacked out- I didn't remember what happened right after we both exploded, but we were both lying on the floor breathing hard. I regained my senses and went to the bathroom and got two more towels and two bathrobes. When I returned to the kitchen, Leslie was still on the floor, out of breath. When I touched her, the only response was to mumble: "no Darius no more... not now my legs feel weak, I don't want to stand right now." I picked her up into my arms went to the sliding glass door leading to the back yard. I struggled with the latch for a few seconds before I finally opened it. I was a bit exhausted myself.

"Where are we going Darius?" Leslie asked in breathless voice. "Relax" I kissed her and walked down the deck, the motion lights illuminating my way and set her down slowly in my marble hot tub. It was already warm. I had hit the heater switch before I went to get the towels and robes. "Leslie, babe how do you feel? I inquired. Obviously she was in total ecstasy. Leslie was leaning against the wall of the hot tub with her eyes closed.

"Okay" she smirked. "I think I'm feeling OK." I slowly eased into the tub, wrapped my arms around her and closed my eyes and let my mind replay every thing that just happened. It couldn't get any better than this. I exhaled and thanked God.

Chapter 19

I woke up to the smell of bacon and as I said before, God knows I love bacon. I looked around the room and noticed that Leslie was gone. I started to get up but realized that I didn't have any bacon in the house. I glanced at the clock; it was past noon. Damn! I never slept this late! I got up to relieve myself; I don't know if it's me but the first piss of the day seems to last for hours. By the time I brushed my teeth and washed my face, I heard the bedroom door open and Leslie say,

"Darius?" I walked out the bathroom and one look at her made all the hormones in my body activate. I was rising to the occasion again. She had on the lingerie I bought for her. It wasn't much, but what little there was, she wore it to perfection. I began to stare incredulously.

"Darius," Leslie repeated. I snapped back to reality. "Get back in bed." She didn't have to ask me twice. I practically leaped from the bathroom door to the bed, sliding over to make room for her and the same time hiding my erection under the sheets. She walked over to me and I pulled me close.

"Leslie, where did you get the bacon from?"

"About ten o'clock, Mr. Johnson came by to talk to you and I was already up getting something to drink. He walked into the kitchen because we left the door open." She read my facial expression.

"Well, no, Darius I had on a robe, for goodness sake! I told him you were still asleep and asked him where the nearest supermarket was. He tried to explain, but said it would be easier to show me. So I went and bought us some food to last us through the day. All you had were a few cans of beans, ice, beer, honey and whipped cream. Very convenient."

My mind quickly thought of what I could do with the honey and whipped cream. I just grabbed and pulled her underneath me.

"Noooooo! Darius. The food is getting cold." She pulled away.

"So what? I'm getting hot," I said. I kissed her neck, her shoulders, working my way down, kissing every inch.

"It's my turn," Leslie stated. She pushed me onto my back, climbed on top cowgirl style and grabbed my erection and looked at me with pleading eyes.

"Darius, I just want to please you. I'll do anything to make you happy but I've never really done this before."

"Then don't." I said coolly. What I really meant was please baby please!

"No, Darius, I want to try. Please bear with me."

I closed my eyes and adjusted the pillow and waited for what seemed like five minutes as she examined every inch of it.

" Leslie, don't. It's not important to me."

"No. Darius, I want to". She tasted me, just a lick at first, then she tried to swallow me and almost choked.

"Leslie., what…"

She rose almost taking an inch of my skin under her teeth. Her eyes were watering and she quickly put her hands to her throat.

"Leslie," I grabbed her. "It's alright. It's not important."

"No, Darius. It's important to me. I'm going to please you totally, so lay back down." I started to speak again.

"Listen…"

"No, Darius lay down." She wiped the tears from her eyes.

"Leslie, let me help you." I lay down and she grabbed by erection again.

"Leslie, imagine it as a Popsicle. Lick the top." She did as I instructed.

"Now, lick around the top slowly with the tip of your tongue." I closed my eyes and leaned back into the pillow again.

"Now lick from the base up to the top, slowly, like when you were a child and that Popsicle was starting to melt. Close your eyes and enjoy that Popsicle. Lick the whole thing. Every side. You don't want to miss a spot and let it drip." She was a quick learner.

"Now slowly put it in your mouth. First think about how juicy that Popsicle is and how much your mouth is watering for it. Now taste it slowly, a little at a time, use your tongue and lips. No teeth. Please no teeth."

Leslie took in the tip several times. Quickening her licks each time.

"No. slowly." It was a slow process at first but she began to taste more and more of me, inch by inch.

"Relax, let your mouth relax and take your time. Now all three steps mix them up. Go from step to step and devour that Popsicle." I leaned back and enjoyed every minute of it. A man knows what he wants, so who's better at teaching than the one whose receiving? I was taken back into a trance for some reason. I thought of Brenda. I think she was the best who ever did it. I was brought back to reality because Leslie had stopped.

"What's wrong?"

"Nothing," she said. I pulled her close and kissed her neck, then her breasts. I turned her over and entered her, as we both worked ourselves into a sexual frenzy. I said the words that I promised myself I wouldn't use until I really felt it, and I think I made the whole experience that much sweeter.

Chapter 20

It had been two weeks since I told Leslie that I loved her. It wasn't because we were enjoying great sex; I really meant it. I know we'd only been together a few weeks but I wanted to be with her every chance I got. What I was experiencing was stronger to me. Love was a big step and I wouldn't say it if I didn't mean it. With Brenda, the word never came to mind. The last woman who I actually told that I love her was Joyce Jones and that was six years ago. There have been at least twenty to thirty women in my life since, but after Joyce, Never again, did I want to seek love.

Joyce was an office manager at a medium-sized law firm in midtown Manhattan. I was still working for Roto Rooter when the firm called because they had a problem with the bathrooms in their office. I was sent in and when I first laid eyes on

Joyce, I was hooked on her eyes, her lips, her thigh and her hips. She was the total package. I walked into her office while she was berating the building's custodial staff. I didn't hear a word she said because I was lost in her beauty. I often daydream when I'm transfixed by a beautiful woman. She stood about 5'6" or 5'7" with the most radiant honey bronze skin. Her eyes were grayish blue and almond shaped. She had a slim Anglo nose and set of soft full lips. She wore a silk blouse that was slightly opened to reveal some cleavage and brown pants that did nothing but accentuate her very round ass.

As she spoke, I stood back and took in every curve of her body.

"Ah, hello, how may I help you?" she asked sweetly.

"Oh, I'm the plumber," I answered.

"It's about time," her attitude instantly changed. She grabbed her jacket to her suit, covering up my view.

"Follow me." She headed out the door and walked down the hallway. I stayed back a few steps so I could watch her butt shake as she walked.

"Excuse me, what is your name?"

"Darius, Miller."

"Well, Mr. Miller, I hope you understand that this is an emergency and I will not have you standing around all day, trying to pay your hourly bill."

"No, ma'am."

"Please don't call me ma'am. I'm not that old. My name is Ms. Jones."

"I'm not trying to offend you, Ms. Jones, but it is the proper way to respond to someone you are not acquainted with. I was just showing you the respect you deserve. As people of color, we need to show each other the proper respect instead of: 'yo', or 'hey Shorty', or 'wassup'? It should be hello ma'am, how are you doing?"

Joyce looked back and smiled. "Okay, Mr. Miller. Thank you for the lesson on culture, but that's not why I called you."

We arrived at the bathroom in question. "This is why we called you" Joyce said pointing to the restroom clog, and turned to leave. I said to myself. What the hell, you can't get them all.

I unclogged the stack line and left the bill with the receptionist. Outside I saw Ms. Jones and another woman in the diner across the street, having lunch. I walked into the diner and ordered a cheeseburger and paid my bill and theirs. I took the receipt over to their table.

"Excuse me Ms. Jones, but lunch is on me. How about lunch later this week?"

Joyce looked at me and said, "Thank you, but I'm not interested. " Her face grimaced as her friend kicked her under the table.

"Hello, I'm Donna, the friend. said" We shook hands as I introduced myself to her.

"Well, enjoy lunch Ms. Jones, and nice to meet you Donna." I turned and walked out.

The next day Joyce called the office and asked me to call her back.

"Mr. Miller, I love would to have dinner with you Friday night."

Friday I got to her house at 7:30p.m. She was dressed but couldn't find a babysitter for her six-year old son, Andrew. Instead of canceling the date, we took Andrew with us to the movies and some McDonalds. I enjoyed both their company and from that night on we were inseparable. We took trips to Six Flags in Atlanta, later to Bermuda, and Jamaica. Within six months Joyce, Andrew and I were living together. I had bought new furniture and fixed up her old house. We went to church every weekend with her mother. I told Joyce that I loved her every day and did everything to show it. I bought her a five-carat engagement ring and we set a wedding date. A month before the wedding, Joyce came clean.

"Darius, I love you but I can't marry you."

The news hit me like a ton of bricks. "What are you talking about, Joyce? If you're nervous, don't worry."

"No, Darius, it's not that. Well...my son's father is coming home from jail and I think I'm going to give him a second chance."

"What?"

I was completely lost.

"Darius please don't be upset with me," Joyce said with tear-filled eyes.

Don't be upset! I wanted to kill this bitch. I quietly got dressed and walked out. Before I got to the door Andrew stopped me.

"Daddy, where are you going?"

I had the little boy calling me 'Daddy'. Do you believe that? In my mind I had two sons.

I couldn't tell him I was going to my truck to get my gun and kill his fucking mother. Shit I'm the only father he had ever known. I don't think that Joyce knows that her son saved her life.

I should thank her because after what she did to me, I put all my time into opening my own business. She's the reason I have everything I own now!

Chapter 21

"Darius what's wrong with me?" Brenda asked. I thought to myself. What is this, some kind of trick question?

"There's nothing wrong with you Brenda. Is this what you brought me out here to ask me? Brenda, I've got work to do."

"No. Darius, please, sit down and talk to me. Tell me the truth."

I sat on the park bench in the middle of Kings Park on Jamaica Ave and Parson's Blvd. Looking at the Q83 bus idling in the distance.

"Brenda, what do you want to talk about?" I was trying to keep the anger out of my voice.

"It's been seven years since we met and all we ever share besides DJ is sex. You have never taken me anywhere, not even to a fucking movie." I started to get up but she grabbed my hand.

"No. Darius, listen to me. Let me get this off my chest." Brenda said sternly.

I looked at Brenda for the first time in years. She was still attractive. She was wearing a jean skirt that came to mid-thigh and a blue pullover silk shirt that I know she has owned for the whole seven years.

"Alright, Brenda. Talk to me. What's on your mind?"

"Darius, why can't we try to work things out and give our son a normal family?"

That simple statement got me pissed me off to the highest degree of 'pissivity'. I took a deep breath and looked her in the eyes as I told her my true feelings.

"Brenda, because I don't love you and I don't want to spend the rest of my life with you."

"I know you're not in love with me Darius, but if you stop running the streets and settle down and give me a chance, you could fall in love with me."

Just then my front pant pocket began to vibrate, ahh! Saved by the cell. "Hello, Atomic Sewer and Drain Cleaning, Darius speaking."

"Hi, Sweetie?"

"What's up?"

"I'm okay. How are you?"

"Fine. May I call you back later?"

"Oh, I'm sorry, baby. Are you taking care of business?"

"Something like that."

"Okay. Tell me you love me."

I was lost. I didn't know what to say. Brenda read the agony on my face and she suspected something because she stood up and walked a few paces then suddenly stopped.

"I'll call you later."

"I'm not hanging up until you say it."

"Tell that bitch you love her and hang up the fucking phone," Brenda said in a low voice.

"Leslie, I'll call you back. Brenda what are you talking about, what's up?"

"Darius, fuck you, you deaf bastard! That phone is so fucking loud that I heard everything. That must be the Leslie bitch that bought DJ that fucking truck. You know Darius, you're so full of shit that it's crazy. No, I'm crazy. All these years and all your bullshit. All I was apparently was some quick pussy. Anytime, day or night. That's all you ever did was fuck me anytime anywhere. I never said no, never turned you down because that was the only connection we ever had. If you called me at five o'clock in the morning because you just left a strip club and your dick was hard, I would get up and come fuck you. If you wanted to fuck in this park, I would fuck you. Anything to please you."

She pinched the bridge of her nose, closed her eyes and held out her hand. You know Darius. I don't blame you. I blame myself."

She walked up to me and tried to slap me with her left hand. I grabbed her hand in midair but she caught me with right hand. I grabbed her wrist after she slapped me. Any man who has been in this situation knows what's next. She tried to kick me in the groin but I blocked it with my leg. No, I would never hit a woman but I shook the shit out of her.

"Brenda, cut the bullshit. I never led you on. I was open and honest with you. I told you I wasn't ready or interested in a relationship."

"So fucking me is not having a relationship? Okay Darius"

She lowered her head and pulled her arms from my grip. She went to her purse on the bench. "I didn't want it to come to this." She pulled out some papers and handed them to me.

"What the hell is this?" I asked.

I went to a lawyer and I'm suing you for palimony. We've been together... no let me rephrase that. You've been fucking me for seven years, which makes us common law husband and wife. In New York I'm not entitled to half, but I'm entitled to more than four thousand a month. I may have been crazy to put myself through this bullshit but I'm not stupid. Darius, not for nothing but tell me how Tracey fits into all this?"

I couldn't speak for a minute. I didn't think she would take me to court but that's no problem. She couldn't ever find out my true income.

"What do you mean how Tracey fits into this? She's like a little sister." I began to sweat, this bitch was crazy.

"Come on, that's bullshit! Every time you got tickets to a Knicks or Jets game, you would take her. You took her everywhere. You even paid for her schoolbooks. She spends more time in your apartment then you do and she spends more time with D.J. than you ever did. The shit that really pisses me off is when I tell D.J. not to do something. He tells me Tracy lets him do it. Are you fucking her too?"

It was at a point where she was annoying the fuck out of me.

"Listen Brenda, I never fucked Tracy and what ever this bullshit is, I'll see you in court." I turned to walk away.

"Darius, just to let you know, I've contacted the IRS and will be sending them a little package if I don't get everything I want." Her statement stopped me dead in my tracks. She grabbed her purse off the bench and left the park in a slight jog still looking over her shoulder. She was bluffing. Plus, she didn't have enough evidence. Or did she?

Chapter 22

I had to have a seat as I read the subpoena. Stapled to the subpoena was an outline of finances. The numbers weren't exact but they were too damn close. Income from Atomic estimated at approximately $75,000 a week after expenses, which added up to a little under 5 million a year. Plus, the buildings that I own added another half million a year, stock, bank accounts, and other assets. Brenda did her homework. At the bottom of the paperwork Brenda was asking for $20,000 a month. This bitch is really crazy. What the hell was she going to do with $20,000 a month? She lives in one of my buildings and didn't have any real bills.

"Son of a bitch! Fuck! Twenty thousand mother fucking dollars!"

An older lady walked by looking at me like I was crazy. I felt stupid so I got myself under control. I was out in public for goodness sake.

My phone rang suddenly. "What!" I screamed.

"Whoa! Darius, are you okay?"

I had to snap out of it. "Yeah, John."

"Darius, you sure you're alright?"

"Yes John."

"Well I seemed to have caught you at a bad time but I thought you should know that Marcia has been running your name through the mud. She's trying to have you arrested on assault charges. On top of that we were at a landlord's association meeting setting up an agenda because we are about to battle the city over rent control laws. Well, she's going after your business. She's trying to shut you down. I thought you would want to know. You know she holds a lot of clout in this city and she's hell-bent on ruining you. Darius, are you there?"

"Yeah, yeah. I'm here. Just lost in thought, that's all."

"Darius, if you need anything I'll be there for you."

"Thanks, John." I hung up the phone and lost it.

"Shit! Fuck! Damn it! I had attracted a little crowd in the park by now. I was kicking up flowers and dirt was flying everywhere. My right hand was sore from punching a tree.

"Sir, are you okay?" A voice boomed over my steady stream of obscenities. I turned about and saw two officers of the

151

law in the ready position. Legs spread wide with their hands on the holstered guns.

"Hell no, I'm not alright!" I screamed.

"Sir, if you would please calm down, maybe we could help you. One of the officers' asked. I kicked the fuck out of a group of flowers scattering dirt and rocks at the gathering crowd.

I'm alright now, officers." I said brushed dirt off myself with my throbbing hand.

"Sir, I'm Officer Williams," the first one said, "and this is my partner, Officer Ortiz. Please keep your hands at your sides. Any sudden moves will be considered as an act of aggression."

"I'm alright. I'm calm."

Officer Williams approached me slowly. He was about six feet tall, dark, with a semi-large African nose and very intense eyes.

"What is your name, sir?" He asked while examining my right hand.

"Miller. Darius Miller."

"What's this all about, Mr. Miller?"

"Just...just having a bad day." I sighed.

"Well, Mr. Miller, everyone has bad days but they don't usually try to destroy a public park and bust up trees. You should get this hand x-rayed. Your pinkie may be broken."

Shit, my day is getting worse by the second. Both of our attention was diverted to Officer Ortiz's steady stream of explicit words to the crowd -dispersing them immediately. He was scanning my documents and looked up with his mouth wide open and his boyish features contorted.

"Shit, Williams, Mr. Miller is being asked to fork up twenty thousand a month in child support."

"Please sit down, Mr. Miller. Shit, I need to sit down too."

Both Ortiz and Williams sat down beside me. Officer Williams read the papers.

"Mr. Miller, it's cheaper to keep her," were the first words out of Williams's mouth, "but I can easily see you can afford it. If you don't want to."

"Well, that's the second problem. There's another woman trying to ruin my business."

"Okay, I understand your dick has got you in more shit than you can handle and it's about to get your ass burned." He stood up, looked at me and said, "Women can't live with them and jerk off without them. "It's your choice. I choose women and all the problems that come with them. Get the hand checked out. It doesn't look like you'll be whipping your monkey with it, so you better make up with those women."

Chapter 23

"Darius, baby what happened to your hand?"

I looked down like I didn't know it was bandaged.

"Nothing, Leslie."

"Darius, forget that macho bullshit. What happened?"

"Leslie, let it go." I looked around the shop. It was almost complete except for adding some paint to the walls.
"It looks great. When are you planning on opening up?"

"Darius don't change the subject. Tell me."

I hesitated and took a deep breath. "I punched a tree." The look on her face was puzzling. I don't know if she thought I was stupid or crazy.

"Darius Miller, why did you punch a tree?" She asked holding up my bandaged hand.

"It's only my ring finger. It's a slight hairline fracture. They put a metal brace around the finger to keep me from disturbing it too much. The extra bandages are for a few cuts. I can take them off any time."

"That's nice to know but that still doesn't tell me why you punched a tree."

I thought to myself, it's none of your business but that's not the way to have a healthy relationship. I have to be honest and open and communicate.

"Alright Leslie, I talked to DJ's mom and she is suing me for child support. Twenty thousand a month."

I told her everything and I mean everything. Leslie's mouth hung open as I unloaded all my problems on her. I had never shared any of this stuff with anyone but Tracy. What was the difference anyway? It's not like I was getting married any time soon. What reason would Leslie have to turn against me? She finished reading the subpoena and Brenda's tally of what she thought I was worth. Her eyes spun up in her head as she was adding up the figures.

"Wow, Darius, you can afford it. Why don't you just give her the money she wants?"

"What? What has she done to deserve twenty grand a month? Not a damn thing!"

I had to calm myself down because I was getting a bit upset with the thought of paying Brenda or should I say her mother.

"Well Darius, she is your son's mother and you did sleep with her off and on for seven years."

The steam was rising up in my head that some started to spill out of my ears. I fought hard to control my anger and tone of voice. I thought Leslie was mocking me.

"Because we have had sex off and on for years doesn't make her worth twenty thousand a month. I don't give a damn what anybody says, no pussy is worth twenty grand a month unless it's lined with gold, fits my dick like a vase and makes me cum all day."

Leslie just stood there with her mouth open.

"I'm sorry, Leslie. I went too far. Let's change the subject."

My cell began to ring. Saved by the cell once again.

"Hello, Atomic Sewer and Drain Cleaning."

"Darius, is everything okay? I got the message you left on my voice mail. What hospital are you in? What's wrong? What happened?" Tracy was ranting a mile a minute.

"Tracy, Tracy. I'm okay. I just hurt my hand and my ego. That's all."

"Darius, you had me worried. I called nearly every hospital in Manhattan, Queens and Brooklyn before I thought about calling your cell phone."

"I'm okay. I'll talk to you tonight, okay."

"Darius, what time will you be home?"

"I don't know."

"Well, never mind. I'll see you later anyway."

"Leslie." I turned to talk to her but when Juice decided to walk in, my day was going from bad to worse, just that fast.

"What happened to your hand, Darren?"

"Its okay and its Darius."

"Yeah, right. I'm bad with names," he said with a smirk on his face.

"Leslie, when are you going to give me the grand tour?" Juice grabbed her hand and put his arm around her waist.

"When it's all finished." She said not moving his hand or his arm as she looked around with pride on her face.

"Our baby girl really put something together here Darren, I mean Darius."

What the fuck did he mean, "Our baby girl"? Leslie finally read the expression on my face and moved out of Juice's grasp.

"No this is all Darius' idea." She said.

Juice looked around. "It's nice but you should have gone with some of the ideas I gave you."

That was it. "Juice."

Before I could get anything out, Leslie stepped in and pushed Juice toward the door. "Juice, we were in the middle of something important. I'll talk to you later." She pushed him out the door.

"I'm sorry, Darius."

"No, Leslie, I'm sorry. Let's just forget it. Alright?"

157

"Alright." She replied.

"Oh, Darius, the reason I called you earlier was to tell you that I'm taking my state board exams Saturday morning at 8:00. This time, I feel so confident and it's all because of you. I know I'm going to pass and to take you out afterwards to celebrate."

"No, Leslie I have a better idea. We will have a grand opening gala to celebrate your passing exam and the new Total Experience Day Salon." My mind started racing. I could put it all together in four days with no problem.

"Hold on, Leslie." I grabbed my phone to call the office.

" Valerie I need you to make some calls for me." I gave her the details and let her get to work. I felt excited and this morning's problems seemed like a distant memory. I grabbed Leslie and kissed her once then twice and the third time I let my lips linger. This is just what I needed, something to get my mind out of its funk. I lifted Leslie and carried her to a massage table. She wore a loose fitting shirt. I ran my hand up her legs.

"No, Darius. We can't do this," she said in between kisses. "The door's unlocked. Someone could walk in." At the same time she was unbuckling my belt.

"Better safe than sorry," I said as I locked the door and turned off the lights. The moon was full but we couldn't get its full radiance because of the tinted windows. By the time I got back to the massage table, I had lost every stitch of clothing. To my surprise, Leslie had done the same and had made a make shift bed out of some blankets and whatever else she found. I didn't care. I just laid her back and made love to her and collapsed in her sweet embrace after we were both spent.

Chapter 24

After being awakened by the knock on the door from the paint crew, we hurriedly got dressed. Damn, it was morning already! I gave Leslie a kiss on the cheek and ran to the store for some mouthwash. I didn't want to assault anyone with my morning breath. When I got back I told Leslie I would talk to her later- I had a couple of things to do. On the drive home my mind was putting together Saturday's event. It would be a great way to jump start business if everything worked out.

Damn!

" Atomic Sewer and Drain Cleaning. Darius Miller speaking."

"Darius, it's me, Barry."

"Well good morning, Barry. I thought lawyers didn't make personal calls. Which reminds me of a joke I heard about lawyers."

"Darius, you don't have any time for jokes. I'm calling to warn you that there's a warrant out for your arrest."

"A what! For what?"

"Assault charges on Marcia."

"You've got to be kidding me. I just pushed her off me. There was no malice intended."

"Darius, you put your hands on her. That's assault in the third degree. It's a misdemeanor punishable by up to one year in jail. And remember there were over one hundred witnesses. Plus, she's claiming injuries. She wrenched her back and went to the hospital. As long as there's a hospital record, they could bump the charges up to Assault 2nd, which is a class C felony and carries a maximum sentence of five-to-fifteen-years."

"Oh boy I don't have time for this- What! Five to fifteen years! Barry stop shitting me."

"Darius, I'm dead serious. Because of your business ties and that fact that you have no record that is unlikely. However, if you went to trial and the Mayor of New York got on the stand and told an all-white jury in that small county that he saw you push her to the ground, Darius, you may have a house in the community but you are virtually unknown. Marcia sits on the School Board and the Planning committee. You're in a lose-lose situation. Also I have to remind you that I can't represent you."

That caught me by surprise.

"Fuck, Barry, you bail on me when I need you the most!"

"Darius, must I remind you that my wife is Marcia's first cousin and I handle all family business? It's not the business part that bothers me I am strange after 20 years of marriage I am still in love with my wife and losing her would kill me.   I hope you understand."

"I understand, Barry. Hold one second Barry" I had to pull over because my mind was going in five different directions at once.

"Okay Barry, what do you suggest?" My whole world was crashing down.

"Darius, you have two choices. You can turn yourself in today and I can set it up. I know a firm in Rockland County that is very good. You will go in front of a judge today and because you don't have a record, they will let you go on your own recognizance and give you a future court date. Then you have to think long and hard if you want to take this to trial. Like I said before, the prosecution has over a hundred witnesses. The odds are not in your favor. What I would suggest is that you wait it out for a few months. Get it knocked down to disorderly conduct, which comes with a reprimand and if you don't get in any trouble within a year, everything will disappear. Darius that's what normally happens but we're dealing with Marcia and she may try to pressure things. This brings us to your second option. Just sleep with her."

I was dumbfounded. "What, Barry?"

"Darius, I know what she wants. I've known her for thirty years. The easiest way to get out of this is to sleep with her a few times until someone else peaks her interest."

"Barry, I don't want to."

"Listen, Darius, she's good-looking, has money and would help your business. Who's it going to hurt?"

This couldn't be happening.

"I'll think about it."

"Good. I'll start setting everything up. I need you up here no later than two o'clock."

"I'll be there. Thanks, Barry. Oh, one more thing, Brenda wants to sue me for child support. Twenty grand a month." Every time I said it, I got pissed. "She also threatened to turn me into the I.R.S."

"Darius, pay her. You can afford it. You don't need the trouble with the Feds. Once they get started with you, it may take years, but they're going to get you one way or another. I know you have bones in your closet you don't want exposed, so give it to her.

"Your right Barr thanks for everything."

Pay Brenda her money. As much as I hated it, it had to be done. First things first, I need to go to my office, handle a few things and then shower and turn myself in.

Chapter 25

When I pulled up to my office, things had gotten worse. Three of my trucks were sitting idle outside. Employees sitting around meant that nobody was making money.

"Valerie, what's happening? Why aren't these guys out doing anything? I was screaming before I had the door fully open.

"Darius, it's slow. Yesterday was even worse. What happened to your hand?"

"I hurt it yesterday. I'm fine, though. What do you mean, it's slow?"

"No work, nothing to do. Mark went by Post Restaurant and saw another company truck outside. He waited around and spoke to a worker. It seems they had a contract with the restaurant group as of yesterday. So we lost our foothold in Manhattan."

"What!"

"Well, that's what I'm told."

"Damn. Marcia is trying to ruin me quick. Shit, my day couldn't get any worse. Val, get me Davis from the group on the phone."

I went into my office slamming the door so hard that it knocked books off the shelves and kicked up dust. I thought to myself that I have to clean this office. My phone started to ring before I had time for my eyes to adjust to the dust cloud.

"Davis, this is Darius Miller from Atomic. What's going on?"

"Darius, I don't know what you're talking about."

"Well, from what I understand, you canceled my contract with the Group." The Group consisted of over 200 restaurants throughout Manhattan.

"No, we didn't. We had another company look over some work and give us an estimate- so when your contract does expire, we can get the best price. Its nothing personal Darius; its business."

I knew he was lying.

"Davis, our contract isn't up for another eight months. Isn't it kind of early to start looking for a replacement?"

"Darius, I want you to read between the lines. I was told from the top to look for a replacement for Atomic. I don't know whom you pissed off but you are going to be replaced no matter what. I don't know what you did or whose toes you stepped on but from what I did gather was they are trying to put you out of business."

"Thank you for your honesty." I hung up the phone.

Before I could process the new data in my head, Valerie was on the line again. "Mr. Miller, there are two detectives out here to speak with you."

"Okay, send them in."

I leaned against my desk, closed my eyes and awaited my destiny.

"Are you Darius Miller?" one of the officers asked. I still didn't open my eyes.

"Yes, I am."

"We have a warrant for your arrest."

I opened my eyes and looked at both officers. "Sir, I know. I have a court date up in Mountainville later today."

"Mr. Miller, I don't know what is going on, but we were told to bring you in for extradition to some upstate county, that's all. Where it is I don't know and don't want to know."

"Wait one minute. If the warrant is not from the city, then why are you here? It's not in your jurisdiction."

"Mr. Miller, don't make this hard. Please come with us and they will explain everything at the precinct." Both officers were older, balding and overweight. One had pinkish skin with close-cropped blond hair mixed with gray. The second officer, who was doing all the talking, was well tanned with all grayish, white hair and strong features like he was fighting his battle with obesity but losing. If I wanted to run there was no way they would catch me but I wasn't running anywhere. I stood up slowly and walked around the around the desk to assume the position. I was searched, cuffed and led out of the office. Valerie was so shocked that the food she was eating fell out of her mouth.

"Darius, what's happening?"

"Nothing I can't handle Valerie. Call Barry Goldstein for me and tell him I was arrested. He knows what to do."

"But Mr. Miller…"

"Valerie, please! I promise I'll explain everything tomorrow. Keep everything under control."

I thought I saw tears welling up in her eyes.

Thank you, Val. Everything will be all right."

Out in the car, tan face turned back and said, "Mr. Miller, I don't know who you assaulted because we usually wouldn't have picked you up on a warrant from an upstate town without one of their officers hand delivering the warrant, but this came from the Plaza. Whoever made this call wanted you picked up right away."

Chapter 26

I was handed off in the parking lot of the 113th precinct like some cheap luggage from a blue Ford Crown Victoria to a dusty gray Caprice classic. Papers were signed on the hood of the car as I sat in it. Something didn't seem right about the whole deal. The two Mountainville Deputies both looked around after the transaction was done at all the black faces that occupied the South Jamaica area as if they never seen so many people of color at one time. They both looked no more than twenty-five.

"Mr. Miller, we are going to rearrange your handcuffs. It's a long ride and we want to make you more comfortable."

Yeah right. When did cops want to make one of their detainees more comfortable? Who was I to complain? Slowly and carefully they rearranged my cuffs from the back to the front and added a chain to the middle, which was welded to the floor.

At least my hands were in front of me and I had some movement.

The two officers didn't introduce themselves so I gave them names. The driver's face looked like it was put together from extra parts from a Mister Potato Head game. So I called the driver "Ears" because one ear was an inch bigger than the other. The other I called "Leatherneck" At his young age, you could tell he spent too much time in the sun. His neck looked like old shoe leather. Neither spoke a word to me for the whole 2 hour ride until we arrived in front of the courthouse in Mountainville and I really mean house. The court was an old, one-story house that was supposed to date back to the Civil War. They took the cuffs off me and led me into what seemed like a walk-in closet with bars, and shoved me in. I waited for what seemed like hours but it gave me time to reflect back and plan a way out of this mess. I could kill Brenda. But I'm no murderer and she's my son's mother. I'm just going to have to pay her and have her sign a contract so she couldn't bleed me. Marcia on the other hand, had me stumped and the only way out of it was to succumb to her wishes. I was startled out of my deep thought by a commanding voice.

"Hello, Mr. Miller. My name is Matthew Hyatt. I'm going to be representing you. Barry Goldstein contacted my firm and gave me all the particulars and I have spoken with the assistant district attorney. They are charging you with class C felony assault."

"What!" That was all I could say.

"Mr. Miller, I already know the whole situation. Ms. Drake is a VIP and they're just trying to please her, but this case has no merit. We'll have to play their game for a few months until they come to their senses."

I just shook my head and thought, "until I sleep with Marcia".

I looked up and saw an old court officer appear at the door. He looked like he started working here when the court opened. He was frail with slumped shoulders and had more hair in his ears than he had on his head. He reminded me of a taller version of Yoda from Star Wars. Standing next to my lawyer, who was at least 6'5", about 250lbs and built like a pro football lineman. The old court officer looked like a corpse that was decaying but moved swiftly for his age. He opened the door and led me briskly down the hall.

The courtroom was a large room in the front. Everything was old Darkwood planks that were well preserved and polished to a high gloss shine. There were two large wooden tables in the middle of the room and a third in front, no doubt for the Judge. To the right were twelve chairs for the jury and to the left was a stenographer's stand and right by the door were chairs for the few people that came to watch the case, if they ever had any.

We were led in by Yoda and told to have a seat. Yoda went and knocked on the door and the judge walked out. We were told to stand again and the Judge was introduced to us.

The judge took one look at me and said, "bail set at fifty thousand cash and a temporary order of protection is to be in full effect. You are not to go within fifty feet of the victim and if you do, make sure you have your toothbrush, because you'll be staying for a while."

My lawyer just sat there and didn't say a damn word. The judge stood up and went back to his chambers. Yoda grabbed my arm and led down the hall. Back in my cell, my lawyer finally found his tongue.

"Mr. Miller before you say anything, let me explain."

"Explain what, motherfucker! What kind of Mickey Mouse bullshit was that?"

"If I told you that the judge was Marcia's uncle, you would've walked into there talking this isn't fair, I want a new judge routine, and messed everything up. I already put in for a change of venue. Once this case leaves county, it will be reduced. All you have to do is make bail and I'll handle everything else."

I forgot about the bail. Tracy! I needed Tracy to get me the money.

"Phone," I demanded. The lawyer was still talking. "Give me your phone."

He looked startled and reluctantly gave it to me. No answer on Tracy's phone. Leslie was my last option. She answered it on the second ring.

"Leslie, I need you to bring me fifty thousand dollars, now."

" Wha- What! Darius, I don't have fifty thousand dollars."

"Go to my apartment and get it."

"Darius, I'm in the shop, and my car is in the shop."

"Drive my truck."

"I can't drive that truck. It's too big. Where are you?"

"Leslie, listen to me carefully. I'm in jail in Mountainville, where my house is. I need you to bring me money for my bail. Take a cab to my office. I have a spare set of keys to my car and apartment. I need you to go into the basement office. There's a safe down there. Take out the money and bring it to me."

Mr. Miller, they're going to be taking you to Ulster County Jail in Ulster County. They should meet you there."

"Darius, I'll get lost. I don't like driving on highways."

I don't care if you take a taxi up there. Just get me out! I'll call my office manager to give you the keys. Please, get me out!"

Chapter 27

The Ulster County Jail was larger and newer, just like any jail on TV. Not that any jail was a good jail. This was much better than the closet they locked me up in. I was waiting in the reception pen and it seemed like no one worked there. Leslie must have walked or gotten a lift on a turtle because she should have been here hours ago. Finally, my name was called.

"No, Mr. Miller you're not being bailed out." The correctional officer looked at me. "Fifty thousand dollars. Yeah right." He said with a smirk. I wanted to knock the smirk right off his face.

I was led to a room where I was strip-searched, de-liced, and hosed off. Within seconds, I was given a bright orange "jumpsuit" with matching socks and sneakers and sent to get a checkup. I didn't know who to be pissed at. Leslie, Marcia, Brenda or myself. After seeing a doctor I was given a bedroll and the top bunk in a room filled with ninety men at five in the morning. I couldn't believe this shit was happening. I made it just in time for breakfast: one box of Bran flakes, one milk, hard white bread and apple jelly. I passed on breakfast and sat on the bunk.

"Miller on the bail out," I heard a voice say. It was after one in the afternoon and a smile started to cross my face until I looked around and saw all the Black and Spanish faces. I thought about the question I had asked Leslie that I read in Black Enterprise. The answer finally made sense. For every man locked in a facility, this all white community gets paid for them living here because they are counted in their census count and that money is being taken out of the neighborhoods they live in and from the people who support them.

Walking out, I felt like a new man. The sun shined brighter, the air smelled sweeter and I had been there less than twenty-four hours. The sight of Leslie standing next to my car made the day complete. My baby came through for me. Maybe a little late but she came through. But something about her was different.

"Hey, baby, thank you." I said before giving her a toe-curling kiss. I pulled her in and released all the tension I had built up the last few days in a single passionate kiss. Then I noticed the difference. "You been smoking weed?"

"Well, nice to meet you, too."

"What?"

"Nice to meet you too, Mr. Miller. Is that the way you greet every woman you meet? Because if it is, greet me again." She said grabbing my hand. The look of confusion on my face brought a smile to hers.

"When did you start smoking weed? What took you so long? Why did you drive this car, and what happened?"

She started to laugh, "I'm sorry. I'm Lisa."

"Who?"

"Lisa, Leslie's sister."

Well at least that answered some questions. "Where's Leslie?"

"She went around front to see if you were getting released."

"Darius! I turned and saw Leslie and Barry walking toward us. I looked back to Lisa.

They looked identical from head to toe. Leslie grabbed me and hugged and squeezed me tight around my neck.

"I'm sorry. They wouldn't take the money yesterday. They needed to know where it came from. I didn't know what to do so I had to go back to your apartment and get your business certificate out of the safe. It's a good thing Lisa was there because I wouldn't have known to do that..." She was rambling on so- I didn't understand a word she was saying.

"And then Tracy came down and called Barry and he arranged everything. I was so scared for you. This was just awful. Was everything okay? You didn't have any problems in there, did you? I'm sorry, baby."

"Its okay, Leslie. Give me and Barry a minute to talk." Barry and I walked across the parking lot.

"So, Barry, why didn't you tell me Marcia's uncle was the judge?"

Barry just shook his head. "Well, technically, he's not."

"What!"

"Well, he's semi-retired. He asked to cover this case for the steady judge. That's why everything happened so quickly. He called some friend in the governor's office. And that's why you got arrested so quickly. I didn't know what happened until Tracey called me last night. Then I checked everything out."

"So, where do we go from here?"

"Well, they're pushing felony charges. So if I were you, I'd call Marcia, ask her to dinner, fuck the shit out her, and afterwards, I would piss in her face for all the shit she put you through."

"Good idea, but she'd probably like it. I think I have a better way to handle it. Thanks for your help."

Barry looked at Leslie. "I see why you don't want Marcia. If I had twins, I wouldn't chance losing them either."

That brought a smile to my face. "No, I'm only with one. Only one"

Chapter 28

The twenty-minute ride back to my house was quiet and uneventful. Almost. Every time I looked in the rearview mirror, Lisa would blow me a kiss. Almost on cue, Leslie would touch my leg or arm and smile.

We pulled up to the front of my home. I was exhausted.

"Darius, are we just going to sit here?" Lisa said, startling me out of my trance. I had my foot on the brake and the motor was still running.

"Damn, this motherfucker is off the charts." She said.

At that point, Lisa's beauty diminished in my eyes. In my eyes, a woman who uses explicit language to describe what she sees and feels lacks command of the English language and to me, that's a turn off.

"Damn, Darius, you going to give me a tour of this bitch or what?" I closed my eyes and put the car in gear and took a deep breath.

"I would love to, but I have some calls to make. I don't mind if you look around by yourselves." I looked at Leslie and kissed her on the cheek. "Show her around, babe." I opened the door and let Leslie begin her grand tour with her sister.

First things first, I needed a real shower and to get things started. After a long hot shower that brought my mind and body back to life, it was time to restore my daily affairs back to normal. Ms. Drake was first and foremost on my list. I walked around my bedroom in my boxer's and tee shirt thinking on how to set everything right. I just couldn't put it all together. Fuck it! I'll just wing it I thought. I grabbed the phone and dialed Marcia's work number.

"Hello, may I speak to Ms. Drake?"

"May I ask whose calling?" the receptionist asked.

I had to think fast because I didn't want to be on record calling her. I would have violated my order of protection and really screwed myself. I dropped my voice an octave, cleared my throat and spoke with a deep smooth Barry White tone. "Yes, this is Mike Smith," I lied.

"We met a few weeks ago. I was out of town and this is my first chance to call since the Johnson's party."

"Please hold, Mr. Smith."

I don't know where the name came from but fuck it.

"Hello Mr. Smith," Marcia said with curiosity in her voice. "I don't recall meeting you."

"Marcia, don't hang up on me. This is Darius Miller."

"Why shouldn't I?" She proclaimed loudly.

"Because you win." It hurt me to say it. "Yes, Marcia, I give up and I'm calling to ask you to dinner Saturday. I have a room at the Plaza Hotel. We could order room service or we can go out to dinner and I could make everything up to you. I'm so sorry about everything and…"

"You're not sorry about shit, Darius. You fucked up with me and didn't realize I couldn't ruin your ass."

I was pissed but I had to hold my tongue. "You're right, Marcia." I said, sounding like a scared little child.

"I told you I get what I want, sooner or later. So dinner and a night at the Plaza – please I'll accept that as a start, but don't think everything will be okay. Afterwards, you'll be playing by my rules and what I want you will give me with no questions asked. When I say jump, don't ask why or how high, just jump and stay there until I say come down. Do I make myself clear? Mr. Miller?"

I imagined myself strangling her. I looked down at the phone and noticed that my hand was wrapped around the phone so tight that it cracked.

"Yes Marcia, I understand." I said through clenched teeth.

"Darius, I don't like the way you said that. Maybe jail will suit you better. So if you want me to give you a second chance… say it with a smile."

"Yes, Marcia," I tried to sound thrilled about spending the evening with her.

"Okay, Darius. I'll see you Saturday at let's say….eight sharp. Oh, about the room; I'll get it. It's not that I don't trust you, well yes; it is that I don't trust you. See you Saturday."

That bitch! Now I had to keep control of the situation. Like I always say, "I have friends and customers all over the city" and the plan I had shaping up, I could still pull off.

Now from annoying bitch number one to annoying bitch number two.

"Hello, Brenda?" I said as soon as she picked up the phone.

"Darius, is everything okay? I heard you got arrested."

"Yes, but I don't want to talk about that. I'm sorry and want to make things right. So if you will have your lawyer draw up the papers, I'll sign them."

"Well, Darius, I changed my mind. I don't want the money."

I felt relieved but something wasn't right.

"Brenda, come again?"

"No, Darius, I don't want the money. After reviewing things further, you're useless to me. You don't own shit."

"What!"

"Yes, after digging deeper, it appears that DJ owns everything and I am his mother and legal guardian. I'm going to take over his affairs, which means the ownership and running of Atomic Drain and Sewers. Why settle for a piece when I can have the whole pie?"

I was completely dumbfounded. "Brenda, you don't know anything about the business."

"I know, Darius. That's why I'm letting you stay on and run everything. I know you wouldn't ruin your son's business."

"Brenda, please hold one moment." I put the phone down and punched a hole in the wall.

Fuck! I re-injured my hand.

"Okay, Brenda, I'm back." I was shaking like a leaf and felt like I was having a nervous breakdown. I broke out into a cold sweat and didn't recognize that my voice was lifeless and hollow.

"Darius, I hope you understand. I still and will always love you. You drove me to this, so you can't blame anyone but yourself. I'll be taking over Monday morning. So I will appreciate it if you clean out my office over the weekend."

"That I…"

"Darius, I have nothing else to say to you except don't be late. Bye."

I don't know why I wasn't as upset with Brenda's bull-shit as opposed to Marcia's. Maybe I knew deep down that Brenda would wise up sooner or later and I knew she was easier to handle than Marcia. I already had a backup plan. I grabbed the phone and called the Plaza. Like I said before, I had an ex-girlfriend who is a manager there. All I had to do was explain to her what I needed to do and she would agree to help. Next, I called one of my customers, an ex-cop who now does security consultation. He directed me to everything I needed. Marcia would be taken care of... finally.

Finally, I had to give Valerie a call. Business was still slow but I didn't really care. She had taken care of all the calls I had asked her to make. From all the positive responses she gave me, Leslie's grand opening was going to be a success.

After getting dressed, I watched Leslie and Lisa sit by the pool. They were mirror images of each other. The only way to tell them apart was that Lisa is left handed. The only way I noticed that is because she was holding a blunt in her left hand. After taking a pull of her blunt, Lisa stood up and removed her shirt and bra, slid out of her skirt and jumped into the pool. I got excited there for a minute. Every man's fantasy is to have two women at once and twins would be like hitting the jackpot in Vegas. Leslie jumped up and screamed at her. I quickly snapped out of my trance. The last thing I needed was more women problems.

Chapter 29

Saturday. D-Day. Everything was set up and ready to go. I should have been happy but all I could think about was the argument I had with Tracy last night at my apartment. She thinks I'm slipping. I let the situation with Brenda get out of control. I let Leslie know too much of my personal life and the fact that I let her into my safe really blew Tracy's mind. She was right but being the always overconfident male that I was I could not admit it and during the argument, though we were at each other's throats, I was somehow turned on by it. After she left and slammed the door behind her, I finally realized how important she was to me.

"Darius, I did it! I did it! I passed, I passed!" I was brought back to reality. I looked up. Leslie was at the passenger side of the car. She had the most beautiful smile I ever saw her wear. Her hazel eyes sparkled in the sunlight; her skin glowed. She was talking a mile a minute.

"Darius, it's all because of you! Today is the best day of my life. I love you so much, Darius."

She jumped in the car without opening the door. I was startled. My first thought was if her performance scratched the paint. I may not have known the name of the color, but I did not want it scratched.

"Darius, Darius, I did it. I did it! I passed. It's all because of you." Leslie kissed and hugged me. The show of affection had me turned on as she touched my legs: first the right, then the left, and then the middle. She gripped the middle one firmly.

"Let's go back to your place and celebrate and I can show you just how good a teacher you are." She licked her lips, unzipped my pants, freed me from my restriction, massaged my penis then leaned back and winked at me. She blew me a kiss. "Come on, Darius. Let's go celebrate."

"Leslie, I'm glad you passed and I really want to celebrate, but the shop opens in ninety minutes and you have to shower and get dressed." I couldn't believe I was turning down sex.

"So, can we go to your house and have a quickie? I'll take a shower there and dress at the shop. My dress is there. Please?" Leslie tilted her head to the side. She squeezed and stroked me, then gave me a kiss on the cheek. I looked at my watch. Fuck it. I started the car, put the top up and took off flying. I made it back to my house in less than ten minutes. We didn't make it to the bed. I had barely closed the door before we got our clothes off.

"How am I doing teacher?" Leslie asked, looking up at me, or should I say down. I was laying flat on my back, enjoying every minute of it. I was barely able to speak. I had to admit she was a fast learner. My mind and body were totally relaxed. I was floating off into another dimension. She stopped and kissed my stomach. She whispered in my year that she loved me.

"Teach me, baby. Teach me to please you," Leslie kissed my forehead, my lips, and my cheek. She sucked my ear. Damn it, she found my spot I almost exploded. I took a deep breath, counted to ten, and brought myself under control.

"Leslie, turn around so that you are facing my feet." She got up slowly and turned. Softly she straddled me. As I entered her, the warmth of her almost brought me to a climax. "Okay, it's all up to you." I said. Work it."

She started to slowly work her body up and down, back and forth, left and right, savoring every inch. "Oh, Darius", she said, increasing speed and grinding down harder. "Oh, Darius," she said again, then stopped suddenly and started to tremble. Oh, Darius, she said again this time moving slow again. Darius she said come with me now she increased her motion then stopped and trembled again. She stayed still for almost a minute then I felt her muscles contract around me.

She lifted herself up slowly and lay down next to me and kissed my ear and cheek.

"Teacher, what was that?" she said, short of breath." I never experienced anything like that." I spoke without opening my eyes, " It's like doing it doggy style but I give you total control because you're on top and it angles the penis right at your 'G" spot." I was proud of myself. As much as I didn't want to we had to leave. "Come on. Leslie, we have to go."

"I can't D, my legs are trembling. Oh, God, that was so good, I can't move right now."

Chapter 30

Where have you been?" Lisa yelled as soon as we pulled up. "And look at your hair! You're not even dressed. Look at your face" she stopped and took a deep breath and looked harder.

"Leslie, you just got some, didn't you?" Leslie and I looked at each other and just smiled. "Oh, you're out getting your freak on and I'm here running your shop. You have people asking for you and I don't know what to say. Why didn't you call and say you were going to be late?"

Leslie just opened the door and walked past Lisa. Lisa stopped ranting and looked at me. And why not! I was looking damn good with a lightweight blue Bill Blass suit, with a silk blend T-shirt underneath, and head freshly shaven, goatee freshly trimmed. I pulled out my two-carat diamond earring and platinum chain, nothing too gaudy. I finished it all off with a pair of dark blue gators. I stepped out of my Benz, stopped, struck a pose, nodded my head at Juice across the street, and looked up at the bright clear blue sky. I didn't walk; I glided over to Lisa. Good sex can change the way a brother walks; it puts a little pep in his step.

"You changed her," Lisa said.

I just smiled." Only for the better," I walked into the shop.

Inside, the shop looked great. The marble floor was polished to a high gloss, the walls were a soft pink and it went well with the gray marble. In the middle of the ceiling was a small chandelier with gray smoked glass tassels. To the right were sinks for facials and three feet away from them was massage chairs for quick back and neck message. And next to those was the full massage table separate by partition and a curtain in front for privacy. Continuing down was the waxing room, then on the left of it was the steam room, big enough to accommodate five people. The glass wall around it was tinted for privacy. There was hardwood floor in front of the steam room, also polished to a high shine. It really looked great. I felt like a proud parent, like I put it all together.

"Darius?"

"Yes, Lisa?"

"I need to talk to you, if you don't mind." Lisa grabbed my arm and pulled me into the waxing room.

Darius, I need your help," she said as she closed the door. She walked over to the table and sat down. She was wearing jeans and Oxford shirt that was unbuttoned just enough so that you could get a good look at her breasts.

"I just want to thank you for everything you have done for my sister. She's much more confident in everything she does. I see you got her into reading and wanting to get involved in political affairs."

I didn't know what to say. I just nodded my head. Lisa walked up to me and hugged me, then kissed me gently once, twice. Then passionately. I responded for a minute, then stopped.

"What are you doing?" I said, breaking the embrace.

"We," Lisa said. "You and me. I hear all the stuff you're teaching her. I just wanted to know if you were thinking of taking on any more students."

I backed up. What the fuck was wrong with women lately? Shit, two months ago I couldn't buy pussy. Now they're all trying to throw it at me.

"Lisa," I said, taking a deep breath. "I love your sister. I would not do anything to hurt her." I thought to myself, five years ago I would have slept with both of them without a second thought.

"So please let's act like this never happened, and make sure it doesn't again." I opened the door and walked out. The place had a few people. Looking around I walked straight into April, Leslie's receptionist, feeling guilty. I wondered if she could read it on my face.

"Hi, Darius," she said, giving me a friendly hug. "The Masseuses are here. They will be giving massages. There's champagne, wine, cheese, and sandwiches on the counter. Please help yourself. Leslie will be with you shortly and I want to tell you, I've never seen her so happy. You are the best thing that has happened to her. I really felt guilty. This place is going to be a success, thanks to you. I wish I could find someone like you. You don't have a brother or any friends floating around?" April smiled to reveal that gold tooth.

"No, I don't, I said.

Just my luck. I keep meeting the wrong type of man." Maybe it's that big gold tooth. I thought Lisa walked by us and smiled. April smiled back. There was no love in her smile. "Well, let me see if Leslie is ready. Oh, Darius, there are two journalists here to interview Leslie, and there is a rumor that Cynthia Davis, the model, is on her way here. Can you believe it?"

Leslie appeared by my side, grabbed my hand and kissed my cheek.

"Thank you again for everything." April kissed my other cheek and walked off. She was wearing the hell out of a jean skirt and was very attractive, but the gold tooth ruined it for her. Leslie grabbed my hand tighter.

"How do I look?" she asked bringing my attention back to her than Lisa came and stood next to her. It started to get hot.

I could feel the sweat dripping down my back. I looked at my watch.

"Leslie, I'm sorry. I have to go."

"Darius, no! You did all this. Stay here and share my day with me, than we can go finish celebrating tonight."

"No, Leslie. I'm sorry. I have a little emergency to take care of."

But Darius, I don't know what to do."

I'm sorry, but I have to go. All you have to do is look beautiful and let people walk around, drink, and eat a little. Just show them what you have to offer. Also, Cynthia Davis is coming and there are a few journalists here to interview both of you. If you remember, Ms. Davis beat Tyra Banks for the cover of the Victoria Secret catalogue and was featured in the Sports Illustrated swimsuit issue. Also Douglas Foster will be here, so you will have the future Mayor of New York. It's the best publicity anyone can get."

"But Darius, I need you here. What would I say or do around celebrities?"

"Just be yourself and everything will be just fine." I kissed her on the cheek. I'm sorry. Tell Douglas and Cynthia I had an emergency and had to run out. I love you." I walked out and jumped in my car. Even with the top down I was still burning up. Fuck, ain't shit going right.

Chapter 31

I got to the Cross Island Parkway with no destination in mind. I just needed to get away from it all and clear my mind. I am a good person. Why was everything getting so fucked up? I looked to the heavens for an answer and almost hit a blue mini van. I had to get it together. I was losing control and being a Leo male, we loved control in everything we do. Marcia, Brenda, and now Lisa, all were chipping at my control, fuck! I looked at my watch. I had two hours before I had to meet Marcia. That bitch! I put in my special mix CD featuring Donell Jones, Musiq Soulchild and Jaheim. I chose the best songs from all their albums. I usually listen to it when I'm upset. It had its usual calming effect on me. I pulled off at Queens Boulevard exit, drove over to the Queens Center Mall and just sat in the parking lot, eyes closed, sorting out my life. Jaheim was singing, "...put that woman first." I opened my eyes. He was right. If I loved Leslie, put her first. Nothing else mattered. I had money, and I had finally found love.

I decided to call up my love.

"Hello? April, let me speak to Leslie."

"Who's calling?"

"It's Darius."

"Darius, are you all right?"

"Yes, Leslie, I'm finally alright. I'm sorry I abandoned you. Please forgive me. I had a lot on my mind lately but I promise to make it up to you, if you will let me."

"Darius you don't have to make anything up to me. I just want to be with you. I'm happy with you and everything you have done for me."

"It will take a lifetime to make everything up to you."

"I love you." That brought a smile to my face.

"I love you, too."

"Darius, your mom and sister stopped by and invited me to dinner tomorrow. She said she was going to call you. I would love to meet your family, if you don't mind." I didn't mind. I thought about my mom always trying to keep a tab on a grown-ass man, but I wasn't mad.

"Listen Leslie, I have some things to take care of. I'll call you when I'm done and we can finish celebrating, if you want." "Yes, Darius," she answered. "I love you."

"I love you, too."

Chapter 32

I walked into The Plaza Hotel a new man. I felt like I was gaining control of my life again.

"Ms. Marcia Drake's room, please," I asked the desk clerk, a pretty blond with startling blue eyes and a pretty smile.

"Are you Mr. Miller?" She asked in a singsong voice.

"Yes," I said, imitating her voice.

"Ms. Drake is in room 307. Take the elevator to the third floor, make a right and it's the fourth door on your left. She's waiting for you."

"Thank you." When I got upstairs the door was slightly ajar. I knocked and Marcia told me to come in. I walked in and closed the door. Marcia was standing by the mini-bar with a drink in hand, hair still wet from the shower, and her robe open to reveal all her assets.

"Darius, I took the liberty of ordering room service. The prime rib special. Would you like a drink?"

"Sure, why not?" The room was bigger than my apartment. The bed was bigger than my bedroom. The closer I got to Marcia, the better she looked for her age. I had to admit her body was in great shape. Maybe under different circumstances I would enjoy making love to her. I stopped in front of her and gently kissed her lips and her neck. I cupped her breasts, the left nipple, and then the right. She tilted her head back, moaned and removed her robe.

"Darius, slow down and take a good look at what you were passing up." Marcia turned slowly, dropped her robe to the floor, faced me again, and then kissed me a little too wet and sloppy. I could tell she had her share of drinks for the day.

"Have a seat on the bed. I'll be with you in a second." I instructed, breaking our embrace. I went to the bar and filled a cup with ice. I reached the bed and laid Marcia back and kissed her neck, cheek, lips and ears. I massaged her nipples between my forefingers and thumbs, wetting them with my tongue between kisses. I worked my way down to her breasts. Her breathing started to quicken. I took an ice cube and massaged her nipples slowly in a circular motion and licked up the water as it melted and started to drip. Grabbing another ice cube, I ran it down her stomach, then across her thighs, licking up the water trail.

I opened her legs and inserted two fingers and slowly stroked her G spot in a circular motion, then reached and located her A spot. With the other hand I massaged her clitoris with an ice cube.

"Darius don't stop! Don't stop! Right there! Right there!" I stopped.

"What are you doing? Marcia yelled.

I stood up and unbuttoned my pants.

"Taste me," I said. "Before I taste you, I want you taste me." Marcia reluctantly moved over to the end of the bed and tasted me. I entered her warm mouth, closed my eyes and let her work me into a slight frenzy. I was enjoying it a little too much. I broke her grip and she looked at me with a startled look on her face.

"Lay back down," I instructed. She responded instantly by moving to the top of the bed, knees bent, legs wide open. I grabbed a small piece of ice and went back to work on her G spot and clit.

"Put it in me, now. Put it in me."

"I want you to beg. Tell me how much you want it."

"I want it Darius, I want it. Please give it to me. Fuck me, fuck me please." I was still working from her G spot to her A spot as she was talking the volume of her voice was going up and down. I rose up and entered her. One long stroke in, she grabbed my waist and held me down while she worked her body underneath.

"Oh, Darius!" She came and wrapped her legs around me with a tight grip as she shook underneath me. I pushed myself off her and turned her around on the bed. I entered her mouth again and let her bring me to a climax. Right before I exploded, I removed myself from her mouth and discharged on the left side of her face. I got up and walked over to my clothes, as she lay back down on the bed, breathing with her mouth open.

"Darius, bring me a towel please." I got dressed, went over to the dresser and picked up the clock radio. I brought it over to the bed, right up to the cum stain on her face.

"What's wrong with you? Pass me a towel!"

"Get it yourself, bitch." She was startled. Her mouth hung open for a minute.

"What's come over you? Are you crazy?" Get me a towel, now!" She glared at me with the veins throbbing on the side of her neck.

"Get it yourself," I repeated.

"You're done, Darius. I'm going to ruin your ass. I'm going to fuck with you so much, when you go to jail it's going to seem like a fucking vacation."

"Marcia, shut the fuck up. I'm not going to jail and you're not going to fuck with me anymore." I opened up the radio and showed her the tape.

"Give me that, you bastard! Give me that."

"Shut the fuck up and sit the fuck down." I backhanded her. I had never hit a woman in my life, but I must admit it felt better than cumming. I stood on the bed and removed another camera from the light fixture. I then walked over to the desk and removed a camera from the picture frame.

"Alright, this is the way it's going to work out. The charges are going to be dropped by Monday at three o'clock, and you are going to start calling everyone you know and tell them to use Atomic Sewer and Drain Cleaning. For the money that I already lost, you are going to write me a check for ten grand, plus another ten for pissing me off."

"I won't give you shit! Fuck you."

"You already did fuck me. You stupid bitch! Now where was I? Yes, make that thirty grand instead and I would like that to be in my office by three p.m. or these tapes will start showing up at the homes of everyone you know. How would Grandma feel about you begging a nigger to fuck you? How would Daddy feel if he sees you with some nigger's dick in your mouth? Would he still want to kiss you?"

Marcia just sat there, staring at me in utter disbelief.

"Don't be so upset, you suck a good dick. You should be proud of yourself." I started to walk out. "Oh yeah, don't think about trying to say I raped you. The room is in your name and I'm on camera signing the guestbook under your name, as your guest. So wipe the cum off you face and nice doing business with you. She picked up the clock and threw it at me.

Chapter 33

With Marcia taken care of I felt great. My life was coming back under control. I hit the radio and the music sounded so much better. I was weaving through traffic in the city without a care in the world.

"Hello. Hey Mom, what's up."

"I just called to tell you I missed you at Leslie's shop and that I invited her to dinner tomorrow."

"Yeah, Mom. She told me. Mom I am about to go into the Midtown tunnel. I will call you in the morning and Mom, I love you!" I needed to tell her that I don't remember the last time I told her.

Shit the way I feel I love everybody. I glanced at the full moon shining bright. The stars were radiant. My phone rang but I had just entered the tunnel. I looked at the caller id, it was Leslie. That brought another smile to my face. I would rush home, wash the scent of Marcia off me and finish celebrating her special day.

As soon as I got out of the tunnel the phone rang.

"Hey, sweetheart, I'll see you in an hour, okay" I said immediately.

"Darius, this is April. You need to get here right now."

"What happened?" My heart started to race.

"I can't tell you on the phone, but you need to get here fast." I could hear crying in the background.

I instantly stepped on the gas.

I pulled up in front of the shop. I didn't remember the drive there, but I made it in record time. I got out of the car and April was by the door. She ran to me.

Darius, she's in her office." I tried to read her face. It was a mix of emotions: pain, worry and fear. It got my emotions flowing. I didn't know what to expect.

"What's wrong?" I asked. April just looked down.

"It's best she told you." I walked through the shop, not knowing what to expect. I had the feeling I was losing control again. I opened the door to Leslie's office. The desk was a mess. The chair was turned over and magazines were all over the place. Leslie was lying on the floor wrapped in one of the blankets she used for our picnic. Her eyes were wide open and she was staring into space. Under her right eye were black and blue marks, her face was tear-stained, and her hair was a mess. I bent over to touch her. She flinched at my touch and curled up into the fetal position, blinked once and started crying again. Tears slowly ran down here swollen cheeks.

"Leslie, sweetheart, what happened?" She said nothing. She didn't respond to my voice. She just stared into space. My heart sank. I didn't know what to say or do.

"Leslie, let me help you to the couch." I tried to pick her up and she started swinging her fists, trying to hit me. She yelled and when I released her, she went right back to the fetal position. I noticed her wrists had scars around them and her forearms were also bruised. I moved the blanket. She was naked. She balled up tighter, not saying a word, just staring into space. She had more bruises on her legs, upper thighs and butt. I was pissed.

"What the fuck happened? Talk to me. What the fuck happened! Leslie opened her mouth but nothing came out. I stopped. "I'm sorry, baby. What happened?" I said in a much calmer reassuring voice. She opened her mouth again but still nothing came out. I covered her up and walked out.

"What the fuck happened?" April closed her eyes.

"Darius, she told me not to call you or the police." She had her arms wrapped around herself tightly as if she would fall apart. Tears started to roll down her cheeks.

"Darius he raped me, too."

"He? Who the fuck is he and what do you mean you too?"

"April looked at me with a look of agony on her face. "He raped me, too," she said, barely audible.

"I'm sorry, April," I grabbed her and held her tight.

I should have told someone. I should have reported him. I could have stopped this. It's my entire fault. This didn't have to happen." She almost collapsed in my arms. I had to keep a firm grip on her and get her into one of the salon chairs.

"April, it's not your fault, it's his fault. He's a sick bastard and I'll take care of him." My mind was going crazy. I didn't know what to do or say.

"Darius, I'm sorry. When I came back in from the store, Juice was walking out from the back with a smile on his face. When I called Leslie and didn't get a response, I went to the office. Her hands were bound; her dress was ripped and hanging around her waist. I cut the ropes and the dress off. All she kept saying was that she didn't want anyone to know, especially you. She begged me not to call the police but I had to do something. I have to stop him. I can't have her go through the same thing I went through. What I've been going through, having to see him every day, having to put up with his smile and hear his snide remarks. I don't know why I didn't kill him myself, but I'm not letting him get away with this shit again."

Chapter 34

"Lay down. Make yourself as comfortable as possible." After spending the night and half of the next day in the hospital, Leslie was checked out and released. Except for the emotional pain of having to relive what happened for the rest of her life, she would be okay. One of the responding officers gave me the name of a good psychiatrist and the doctor also recommended one. April was given a sedative to try to calm her down because she just lost it. I believe she also would benefit from the help from a good psychiatrist. It seemed that my man Juice was so used to raping men in jail that he lost sight of how to pleasure a woman. Both Leslie and April had been sodomized.

All that good pussy wasted.

I looked down at Leslie. My beautiful angel's face was puffed up and bruised. I didn't know what to say or do to make her feel better. I covered her up and watched her rest for a few minutes before I walked out and let the homicidal thoughts and desires take over my mind. I had already called Paulie and he was checking with some friends about Juice's whereabouts. What I would do when I found him was one of those moral dilemmas that I couldn't answer until he was in front of my face. I could hold my own but I'm no killer. And if I did kill, what if I got arrested and went to jail? I would lose everything and who's to say Leslie wouldn't leave me for someone who's free? I would look like the world's biggest jackass.

Chapter 35

"What is this, Darius?" Brenda walked into my office. I had my executive board members waiting. Shana, my niece, who is the President and Michael, my nephew the Vice President. They were both sitting on the couch. Michael had on a suit, tie and miniature briefcase. Shana wore a two-piece business suit with a blouse and pearl earrings. She had her legs crossed and her hands in her lap.

"Well, Brenda, I have bad news. Business has been bad the past few weeks and the board has gotten together and decided there needs to be changes. You know, a shake-up, and I'm sorry to inform you that Darius Miller the Second has been voted out by the board.

"Yep, Shana said DJ has to kick rocks. He's out of here." I looked at Shana. She smiled. Her deep dimples and caramel complexion made her look like a little angel. She's going to break hearts someday when she gets older.

"Yes, like Shana said, Darius Miller II has been voted out but we have come up with a generous buyout package that will allow him to live the lifestyle he has become accustomed to. Being that you are his legal guardian, we would like you to look over these documents immediately and if you try to fight this issue, then Atomic Sewer and Drain Cleaning will be put up for sale and the business will be dissolved. I must say, there is no market out there for a sewer and drain cleaning company, so everyone loses."

Michael got up from the couch opened his briefcase and handed Brenda the documents and sat down.

"Well, Brenda, you have five minutes to decide what you want to do. Basically, this is the offer: Darius Miller II will receive five thousand a month until he is twenty-one and you his mother and legal guardian, will have control of it. Do you understand the terms of this contract?"

Now Brenda's face was red. Her eyes were like slits. Her upper lip had teeth marks and a trickle of blood on the left side from chewing on her lip so hard.

"Brenda you have four minutes to decide." I said. She shook a little, walked to the desk and signed the papers.

"Thank you for doing business with us. Your first payment will be in the mail in a few days."

She stood and starred at me shooting daggers at me with her eyes.

"Oh, and Brenda, if you deliver that little package to the IRS you get nothing. So for your sake and mine, I'll pick it up from your house. Let's say six o'clock. So get the stepping." That was Shana's favorite line and it brought a laugh from her and Michael and pissed Brenda off more. She slammed the door on the way out. Now, to get my executive committee back to the babysitter.

Chapter 36

"What the fuck, Leslie?" Leslie stood in my door laughing. "Shit, you almost scared the shit out of me. Are you trying to give me a heart attack?" She just laughed harder. "You can't be jumping out from behind doors yelling 'BOO', like you're some five year old."

"I'm sorry. Did I scare the poor little baby?" She kissed my cheek. I went from fear to anger to surprise in thirty seconds. It took me that long to realize that this was the first time that she had been out of the bed in two weeks. Shit, I didn't even remember her going to the bathroom.

"Are you alright, Leslie?" I looked at her like she was a million piece jigsaw puzzle.

. "I'm fine," she said and kissed me again.

"Leslie, I'm glad to see you're up and around, but you're sure you're okay?

"I'm okay, Darius. Believe me; it's all behind me now. I don't want to talk about it, plus I'm starving; so while you shower, I'll cook."

I stood there in a daze. She hadn't said a word to me in two weeks and now she acted like nothing happened. She walked over to the CD player and dropped in a R. Kelly CD and danced off toward my kitchen. Her physical scars had healed and her emotional ones were not far behind.

"Darius, what would you like to eat." She woke me out of my daze.

"Anything babe. Anything you want." I couldn't understand it but I was glad she was all right.

I showered, dressed in an old pair of sweat pants and a T-shirt. I went back to the kitchen to the smell of bacon and God knows I love me some bacon. The table was set with bacon, eggs and pancakes. I looked at her, puzzled.

"Tracy said this was your favorite meal."

"Yes, it is, but when did you talk to Tracy?"

"She came by every day to check up on me." That was new to me because Tracy refused to speak to me. I sat down and just watched Leslie put the finishing touches on the meal. She was wearing one of my tees as a dress and she looked damn good. She sat down, said grace and started eating.

"So, Darius, when do you have to go back to court?"

"I don't. All the charges have been dropped. Why or how, I don't know. Maybe Marcia came to her senses and let everything go."

"What about Brenda?"

"I took care of that also. I gave her the money she wanted."

"Well, Darius I think I'm going back to work tomorrow. I talked to April. Her and Lisa said I should take more time off. They have been doing a good job running the shop without me, but I need to be there. I want to be there. They said you been there a lot also. So, thank you again for everything, but I need to step to my business."

"I think you should take another week off and see that psychiatrist," I said but she just waved me off.

"How do you know Cynthia Davis and Douglas Foster?" She put another piece of bacon in her mouth.

"Well, Cynthia I know through her boyfriend, Nino. Nino Russo you probably read some articles about him and how he's burning up Wall Street. And Douglas Foster I met doing work for his father years ago when he was playing basketball for the Denver Nuggets. Don't be surprised if he wins the mayoral election next year. He keeps saying he's not going to run, but I happen to know for a fact he is. Anyway, Leslie, we need to talk about you."

"Later. There's something else I want to do." She stood up and removed the T-shirt. She walked over to me, firm breasts bouncing, and nipples hard as boulders. She walked behind me and pulled my chair away from the table, came back around, pulled the top of my sweats down, freed me from my restriction and straddled me.

"Leslie, no." She came down on me and wiggled a little to get it all in. "Leslie, I don't think you're ready for this."

"Shh, Darius. I am ready. I know damn sure. I'm ready, willing and able."

But I was not sure about her.

"Leslie, I want it but you need time to let the wounds heal. Let's not rush into this."

She smacked me open-handed. I sat there mouth open, dumbfounded. "If you don't want me no more, just say it. What am I, tainted? I can't take back what happened and now you don't want to make love to me."

She jumped up and ran to the bedroom and slammed the door.

"Leslie, open the door. It's not that I don't want to make love to you. It's just that I don't want to hurt you. I think you should see someone first."

"Oh, now you think I'm crazy! You don't want to fuck a crazy woman!"

"I didn't say you were crazy. I said we should take our time."

"Fuck you, Darius! It's because of what happened. I know it. I've been in bed for two weeks and you've been sleeping on the couch like you didn't want to touch my body." She cried

"Leslie, please, I was giving you time to get it together."

"See? You think I'm crazy."

"Leslie, that's not what I mean."

"Then what do you mean?"

"I wanted to make sure you were okay mentally and physically."

"See, you went back to me being crazy. I am all right mentally and I wanted to make love to you and you pushed me away. Answer that damn phone!"

I didn't even realize that the phone was ringing.

"Hello?"

"Hey D, I found that package you were looking for. Meet me in twenty minutes at the scrap yard on 150th, off Liberty Avenue."

"I'll be there." I hung up and went back to the bedroom door. "Leslie, please open the door so I can get dressed and we can talk about this when I get back." She opened the door, looked at me with eyes red and tears staining her cheeks. She walked to the bathroom and slammed the door.

Chapter 37

I walked into the scrap yard and the first thing I noticed was the trail of blood across the office floor. I followed it to the back of the office. Paulie was on the phone with his feet on the desk. He held up his finger to say he'll be with me in a minute. I looked around the office and it was a mess. There was paper everywhere. The computer looked greasy. The coffee machine sat on top of a mini refrigerator and both had grease hand prints. The floor, which was a thin brown commercial carpet, was matted down with large black oil prints. The walls were wood paneled with pictures of naked women and the snap on tool girl of the month, a big bust blonde holding a socket wrench wearing dental floss as a G-string.

"Yeah, D, he's out back." Paulie jumped out from behind his desk. He had to be two seventy-five easy but he was quick on his feet. We went back to the front where I noticed the blood stained linoleum tile. It must have at one point been white but now it's a dirty gray. We walked out a side door to the yard. The yard was brightly lit. Cars were stacked three high on top of each other in different stages of decay. I noticed Juice was handcuffed to an old Chevy station wagon door handle naked. His face swollen. His lips were swollen and split open. His eyes were beat shut. I walked over to him. He was bleeding from everywhere.

"He's all yours, D." Finish him off."

I looked back at Paulie, who was dressed in all black. He added a pair of black leather gloves to his ensemble. I looked back at Juice.

"Yeah bitch, finish me off," Juice said. As he spoke blood dripped down the side of his mouth. I had to lean in to hear him. I just shook my head.

"You don't have the heart. I knew you were a pussy the night I met you. Leslie put up a better fight than you ever would. Next time you fuck her, all she'll think about is me, bitch."

I turned and swung with all my might. I felt the bone around his left eye shatter. Juice let out a primal scream and slid down the car door. Now I hate to kick a man when he's down, but I kicked the shit out of Juice several times, mostly to the face and ribs. I finished breaking what Paulie had started. He was laid out flat on his stomach and that's when I knew when enough was enough. Juice had a big pink dildo shoved in his ass. It was about three inches around, well, at least the part that was visible. Paulie walked up to me.

"Ribbed for his pleasure, lubricated with crazy Glue." Paulie pulled out a nine-millimeter and handed it to me. "Finish him, D." I took the gun and pointed it at his head.

"Do it. He'll snitch if you don't do it. If he lives; we can't leave a witness. I did fifteen straight; I'm not going back. Finish it." Paulie encouraged me. As much as I wanted to I couldn't do it.

"Yeah bitch, do it. Finish it, you fucking pussy," Juice taunted. I pulled the trigger and hit him in the shoulder, dropped the gun and walked into the office. I sat on the desk. I'm not a killer, no matter what.

"D! Get back out here!" Paulie called from outside. I hesitated. "D!" Paulie called. I walked back outside. Paulie had brought a woodwork table over to the car. He had helped Juice to his feet.

"D, don't worry about it. Everyone's not a killer. It doesn't make you less of a man in my eyes. So I decided to give our man here a chance to live." He pushed the table in front of Juice, grabbed his penis and placed it on the table. He went in a toolbox and got a hammer and three two-inch nails.

"D hand me the duct tape out of the tool box." I tried but couldn't move at first but when he asked again, I finally got my feet to respond. I threw him the tape and he put some over Juice's mouth. I finally realized what he meant to do.

215

"No, don't do that! Oh, God," I yelled as Paulie drove the first nail into Juice. The tape muffled juice's screams and Paulie drove the second one in. I fell to the ground grabbing my own genitals. Juice was out cold on his feet.

"D hand me that gas can." I was still on my knees balls in hand, sweating, crying and scared to death. I was a witness and Paulie didn't want to leave any witnesses.

"D pass me the gas can." I struggled to my feet staggered to the toolbox and grabbed the gas can. I staggered back to Paulie and reluctantly handed it to him. He had his nine tucked in his belt.

"Step back D." He splashed gas all over the car and Juice, and the area around him. Paul smacked him around a few times. When Juice responded he whispered something in his ear and uncuffed him.

"D, hand me the knife from the tool box." I looked at him. What the fuck was he up to now?

"D hand me the knife I said!" I got the knife, a cheap butcher's knife. He set it down beside Juice, set the car on fire and stepped back.

"Let's go." I ran past Paulie and was in my car pulling off as he came out the office.

* * * *

I looked around my apartment. Leslie was gone. She was gone. No note no nothing. I called but I got no answer. I took a shower and laid down. What the fuck was going on?

Chapter 38

"Mr. Miller, Mr. Mingo is here to see you.

"Just give me a minute, Valerie. Then send him in."

I ran to my couch on the left side and got my bat. I don't know why. I ran back and sat behind my desk.

"Good morning, Mr. Miller," Paulie said.

"Paulie don't you think that shit last night was overkill?"

Paulie walked over and carefully sat in the chair in front of me, as not to break it. He leaned back in his chair, looked up at the ceiling and looked at me.

"You know, when I went to prison, I thought I was a tough guy. I had shot this guy over a drug deal. I thought that since I had killed someone, they would respect me in jail. It turned out that all I was around was killers that were tougher then me. I had to fight to keep my commissary; clothes. I had to

218

prove myself and earn respect. I stayed to myself after the first year. My little brother came through the system after me. He ran with Juice and his gang. I tried to talk to him, but he wouldn't listen. Well, some drug money got fucked up and Juice blamed it on my brother. That night he paid off a C.O. and got him and three other guys into my brother's cell. They raped my brother and shanked him. Juice swore up and down he had nothing to do with it but I knew better. " Paulie's voice trailed off and tears ran down his face.

Last night, I just lost it. Don't worry; I'm not mad about you running out on my killing. It isn't easy to do but God is forgiving and I hope He forgives me for what I've done." He leaned back in his chair. A smile suddenly appeared.

"Did you know that the stupid bitch cut his dick off and crawled away?" They found him a block away this morning. Listen, I'm sorry I put you through that madness last night, but it's over."

Paulie stood up. I stood up and walked around the desk. "No, thank you. You did the things I wanted to do but wasn't able to." I gave Paulie a hug.

"D, you and Leslie make a nice couple, but I always thought you would marry Tracy."

No, she won't talk to me, but thanks again." I hugged him again. We both had tears in our eyes.

Chapter 39

Buzzzzzzz! I looked at the clock. It was three thirty in the morning. The bell rang again. I stumbled in the dark to find my way to the bathroom to take a quick swig of mouth wash to answer the door. I opened the door and Leslie was standing there with her head down.

"You can't call or leave a note? I'm just supposed to worry?" She didn't say a word, just stood there with her head down. She was wearing a jacket that came down to mid-thigh and some slippers.

"Leslie, are you alright?" Still she did not respond. She pushed me aside and came in. She opened her jacket and revealed that body that I had come to love so much. She walked over, knelt down on both knees and tasted me. My anger and tension drained away. I came within seconds. She pulled me down to the floor and motioned for me to lie down on my back. I did so, adjusted my position and watched her work at bringing me back to life. After I was fully erect she caressed the shaft from bottom to top and side to side. She worked around my testicles, up my right leg to my stomach left nipple then right my neck my ear. Damn she hit my spot. She pulled her body up and she straddled me slowly bringing herself down then raising back up to the very tip and then coming back down again slower. My nerve ending were tingling. I tried to grab her waist and bring her into me to gain control but she pushed me hand out of the way and continued to work her magic. She put her hands on my chest leaned forward raise her ass changing the angle so with every stroke I was stimulating the clitoris with direct contact. Somehow she contracted her vagina walls and formed a vise like grip on my penis that sent sparks exploding behind my closed eyelids.

"Don't stop, I screamed. Don't stop."

"That's right. Don't stop on my account."

I opened my eyes the only light in the place was coming from the open doorway where Lisa stood. Leslie jumped off me and Lisa walked over to her and hit her with a right cross that would have made George Foreman proud. Leslie stumbled into the coffee table and fell with a thud. I looked at Lisa in horror.

"What the fuck are you doing here?"

"What the fuck am I doing? What the fuck are you doing, fucking my sister? That's probably why you didn't want me the other day. You probably just got finished with her." I got to my feet. I was lost and dazed.

"What the fuck are you talking about?"

I walked over and turned on the light. I looked into what I thought was Lisa's face and realized it was Leslie. I looked across the room and Lisa was slowly getting to her feet.

"Leslie, I thought she was you."

The look on her face was pure evil. "How the fuck did you think that was me, Darius? How the fuck? I have a black eye and she doesn't, so how the fuck could you confuse us?" Leslie took a step closer to me then my mind exploded. I was blinded briefly. I fell to my knees and reached between my legs. I felt like she kicked my balls into my throat because I felt something clog it. I cried out in pain, wiped the tears from my eyes and yelled, "Leslie, I swear to God, I thought she was you! I swear! I'm sorry." I cried. Leslie turned and walked out. What the hell was going on, my mind raced with a million thoughts. I followed her, barefoot and bare-ass naked. "Leslie, I'm

"So sorry." I hung on to the car door while she started the engine.

"You are sorry and you're going to be sorrier when I'm done with you." When she pulled off I had to fight to keep my balance. She got half way down the block and I saw her brake lights then reverse lights. I felt relieved. I thought she was going to give me a chance. She made a quick U-turn, pulled up with a few feet of me and stopped. I started to walk over to the car when she hit the gas trying to run me over. I had to dive for the sidewalk.

I walked back to my apartment feeling like an extra from a Tarzan movie; brushing pebbles and twigs off my ass, dick swinging in the wind. I had forgotten about Lisa. She was sitting on my couch with her jacket on but unzipped, legs wide-open, ice applied to her eye.

"I guess we look alike again."

"Lisa, get the fuck out!" She didn't move. "I said get the fuck out!" She looked at me like she didn't understand what I was saying. "What the hell's wrong with you? Bitch! Get the fuck out."

"Darius, I'm much better for you. I showed you that a little while ago. We'd be good together. I know how to keep a man like you happy. A woman like me could take care of your every need."

I walked over to her and picked her up by the jacket, looked at her and shook my head. The anger was boiling my blood was so hot I could feel it flowing through my veins.

"I said," through clenched teeth, "What the fuck is wrong with you? I not only meant Lisa- I had weeks of pent up frustration from Brenda and Marcia.

"Get the fuck out now or you'll be leaving in a body bag." I had reached the point now I couldn't reach a day before. I could have snapped her throat. I picked Lisa up with one arm walked over to the door and dropped her outside and closed the door. I walked over to the couch, the cold leather biting my ass.

Chapter 40

I don't know how much time passed but Tracy was standing over me, shaking her head.

"Don't you think you should put some clothes on and go to work?" She picked up the boxers, I was wearing when I opened the door last night or earlier this morning, between her thumb and forefinger, extended her arm holding them as far away from her as possible.

"At least put these on."

I slipped on the boxers on.

"Tracy, get out. I don't want to hear it."

"Hear what, Darius? Hear what? Hear about how stupid you looked chasing Leslie around outside butt ass naked? That's what you don't want to hear about. You don't want to hear about how stupid you've been when it comes to women. Well,

you need to hear it." She sat on the couch and faced me. I just leaned back and closed my eyes.

"Tuck that in, please," she said.

"What?" I had slipped out of the opening of my shorts. I groaned and adjusted myself. "Alright, Tracy. Get whatever it is off your chest."

"First, thank you for the show last night. You made yourself look like an absolute fool- an ass!" I was starting to get pissed again.

"Darius, you are a very handsome man and any woman would be lucky to have you and there are a lot out there who want you. Half the women on this block, married or single would love to have you. It's hard to find a good black man with his own business who's not gay. What I'm saying Darius is that you can have any woman you want and all you ever want to do is try to make the perfect woman. You can't keep finding these nuts and try to turn them into the perfect women. It's not going to happen. Only God can create a woman, so let God do His job and wait till He sends the one who's a perfect match to you. Until you realize that, you're always going to end up like this.

"Tracy, are you done?"

"Yes, I'm almost done but let me tell you this. The perfect woman for you has been with you the whole time. You've just been too busy to notice me."

I opened my eyes and looked at Tracy for the first time as a woman. She had tears in her big brown eyes.

"Yes, Darius I've been here for you always. Waiting for you to realize that I'm The One. I loved you from the day I met you. I'm not waiting any more. As a matter of fact, I'm the best thing that's happened to you but you've been too stupid to realize it. It's up to you. You can sit and worry about Leslie, or you can get you shit together and maybe I can help you get your sorry ass back together." She stood up, leaned over and kissed my cheek.

"I'm not going to wait much longer." She turned and walked out. I sat on the cough for the next three days, reliving my entire life and all the women I've ever been with. Actually, if it weren't for the feds coming to my house with a search warrant, I probably would have stayed there another week.

Epilogue

Yeah, that's right. Leslie used everything I told her against me. That's why I'm about to get three damn years. It was my fault. I admit I never should have told Leslie about the package Brenda had put together because as much as Brenda knew, she still didn't have the smoking gun and that was the second set of accounting books in my safe. See I had a little practice of telling people if they pay cash, I would pay the tax and what I did was pay the tax no mind. Leslie came across the books and actually put it together. I guess I was not as smart as I thought I was. I fought the case for two years and the best I could get was three years but I'm not mad because I have the best lawyer any man could have, my wife. Yes, I married Tracy and we have a one-year-old daughter and I also adopted her brother, Marcus. Her mother is still around somewhere. She comes around from time to time for money but we haven't seen her for months. Brenda is a little upset because she quit her job when she thought I was going to let her take over the company and once the IRS got into everything the business folded. She had to go beg for her job back. DJ lives with me, Tracey and Marcus but I still send Brenda money, but nowhere near the five thousand. Marcia, on the other hand, has been bad mouthing me around the city until the tapes started showing up with my face deleted out. So she moved to Florida and hasn't been heard from since. I looked across the courtroom at Leslie. Like I said before, she was one of the most beautiful women I know, but I can't wait to see that smile wiped off her face.

"The court will now come to order," the court officer announces. Case number 992351, State of New York vs. Darius Miller," the Bailiff said. The judge was young, maybe in his late thirties, slightly balding on top, large nose and mustache looking like the novelty set I used to buy when I was younger.

* * * *

Mr. Miller would you please stand. Mr. Miller did you willingly defraud the United States government out of 25.5 million dollars?" He had everyone's attention.

Yes, sir."

"And Mr. Miller, you have pleaded guilty to all charges."

Yes, sir."

"I now sentence you to three years in prison." I looked back. Leslie was smiling.

"Mr. Miller, do you understand that these are serious charges set against you?"

"Yes, sir."

"Well, Mr. Miller I'm suspending those three years and placing you under supervised probation." I turned back to Leslie. That smile was gone and she was up and on her way out of the courtroom. "Mr. Miller, we are giving you a chance to pay the back taxes and fines within ninety days, or you will serve every day of the sentence."

"Yes, Your Honor."

"Okay, case dismissed."

I walked out the courtroom proudly holding my wife's hand followed by my family and Paulie who's been like a brother to me since the night of the Juice incident.

* * * *

Twenty –five million dollars. I know that's a lot of money but once I closed Atomic Sewer and Drain Cleaning I opened Elite Sewer and Drain Cleaning and transferred the ownership of my buildings to Tracy Ann Miller, my wife. Last but not least there was the issue of Leslie and Lisa Simmons. Revenge is a bitch. I bought the building where Leslie's shop was located and as of two o'clock today, I'm canceling their lease. And I happened to have a friend at Washington Mutual Bank and I bought the mortgage on her home. It just so happens that Leslie's a few months late. I think it's time to foreclose.